ESTY'S
GOLD

For Joanna, with love

First published in Great Britain in 2009 and in the USA in 2010 by
Frances Lincoln Children's Books, 4 Torriano Mews,
Torriano Avenue, London NW5 2RZ.
www.franceslincoln.com

British Library Cataloguing in Publication Data available on request

ISBN 978-1-84507-965-9

Set in Ehrhardt MT

Printed in the United Kingdom by CPI Bookmarque, Croydon

1 3 5 7 9 8 6 4 2

ESTY'S GOLD

MARY ARRIGAN

F

FRANCES LINCOLN
CHILDREN'S BOOKS

Alannah is an affectionate Irish term of endearment for a young girl. *Da* is an old word for 'daddy'.

Sometimes, if I close my eyes and think really hard, I imagine I can smell Mama's old sideboard and see again the carved flowers and twisty pillars. But if I linger too long over the memories stirred by the scent of beeswax and old wood, the other smell intrudes, the one that makes me cold and turns my thoughts to cheerless grey – the front-door smell of pale, damp people and poverty.

It was always my chore to dust the sideboard's dark oak surface and rearrange the china ornaments. I had to stand on a chair because I was small for my age and the sideboard was high. There was a mirrored back, which I'd look into and pretend the other me was part of another, brighter, magical world on the other side...

PART ONE
Ireland, late 1840s

Chapter One

I could see them through the parlour window, their ragged clothes flapping against their skinny legs.

'They're back, Mama,' I cried. 'Those children and their mother are back.'

Mama joined me and shook her head sadly. 'The poor things,' she sighed. 'What's to become of them? I'll get some eggs and bread. No, Esty,' she said, as I stepped down from the chair I was standing on, 'You stay here. I'll deal with them.'

'Why, Mama?' I asked. 'Why do you always send me away when they come begging?'

'It's better this way,' she replied, closing the parlour door behind her.

How was it better? I wondered, as I went back to work.

'They're hungry, Esty,' Mama said to me, when the ragged people first began coming. 'The potatoes are rotting in the ground and they have no food.'

'I wish they wouldn't come,' I said. 'They're stealing all Papa's time.'

'Shush, child,' Mama looked shocked. 'You don't really mean that.'

But I did mean it. I was used to people calling on Papa to pay the rent. But that was before the Hunger, when they were just calling to pay the rent. Papa was the middleman for Lord Craythorn who lived in London, over in England. It was his duty to oversee the letting and sub-letting of land, because most Roman Catholics weren't allowed to own their homes and farms.

'But we're Catholics too,' I said to Grandpa one day. 'And we have a lovely farm.'

Grandpa smiled and shook his head. 'We do,' he said. 'And that's because your Papa has an important position. But we don't own it, Esty. We are tenants of Lord Craythorn, just like everyone else who works on the estate. Most English landlords have an agent as well as a middleman, but His Lordship thinks so highly of your papa that he's put him completely in charge.'

Sometimes, of late, Papa said he wished Lord Craythorn would come back to his estate and run it himself. But Mama said he should be pleased that His Lordship trusted him with such important duties. Some days, during the time of the constant callers, I scarcely saw Papa at all. At night there were whisperings and subdued conversations between Papa, Mama, Grandpa and some of the farm workers who lived on the estate.

And then, one drizzly day, some people took a huge pot in a horse and cart up to the Big House.

'Is it a witch's cauldron?' I asked Mama.

'It's for soup, Esty,' she replied. 'We're going to make soup for the poor.'

'Does that mean they won't be calling at our house any more?' I asked.

'I don't know, Esty,' Mama replied. 'We'll just have to see what happens. These are not good times.'

After that, the Big House kitchen was filled with high-born ladies who bustled about and gave orders. I resented the way they spoke to Mama as if she were some servant. *She's the middleman's wife*, I wanted to shout at them. But Mama just went along with their requests. I used to watch the quiet, defeated people line up for the watery soup. It made me feel very lonely because I couldn't relate to them; nor could I relate to the bossy ladies who shooed me away from the kitchen. When Mama said nothing in my defence, but looked at me with sad eyes as she wiped her hot forehead with the back of her wrist, I knew that she was defeated too.

When I asked about the smaller dinners Mama was serving up to us, Grandpa looked annoyed.

'You are fortunate, Esty,' he said. 'Those tenants out there have nothing to eat but the seedling potatoes for next year's crop.'

'Why?' I asked. 'If they do that, Grandpa, then they'll have no crop next year.'

'Precisely,' Papa put in. 'The poorer tenants – the cotters with the smallest bits of land – have nothing left. Why else do you think your Mama is over at the Big House every day distributing soup?'

'Well, why don't they eat their pigs and sheep, just like we do?' I went on.

Grandpa shook his head and frowned. 'They've lost

their animals,' he said, looking at his plate, as if deciding whether to eat or not. 'Nothing left.' Then he speared a small bit of smoked bacon.

'Lost, Grandpa? How can they lose…?'

'Esty,' Papa said, 'they've had to sell their livestock for rent money – and now that's gone. On some other estates the tenants have even had to hand over their animals *in lieu* of rent to the landlords. Their livestock has been rounded up and exported. They say it's happening all over the country.'

'That's bad,' I said, cutting the fat from my smoked bacon and giving it to the cat.

But, I thought, everything would be all right. Bad things get better, like head colds and the blisters from new shoes.

I took to sitting on the Big House steps, watching the ragged, hungry people walk barefoot up the avenue to be fed.

'They wouldn't dare walk up the avenue if His Lordship was at home,' Grandpa said. I couldn't tell whether he was pleased that they were bold enough to do this, or whether he disapproved. Sometimes it was hard to know what he was thinking. Grandpa went to town every market day in the pony and trap. I wished he'd take me with him, but he never did. When he came home, he'd bring news of what was happening beyond the estate, but he seemed to save most of it for when I was in bed, because I could hear the murmurings downstairs.

Often they'd glance in my direction, those pale people, and I'd look away, cross because they were the ones who took up Papa's time, and cross with myself for thinking like that. I wished they'd go away. And then I'd feel confused and angry with myself again.

One day, a woman led a girl of about my own age to the lowest step.

'Wait for me here, child,' she said, and looked at me with an expression of tired defiance, before shuffling around to the kitchen. I looked at the girl for a few moments as she gathered her ragged skirt around her grubby legs. Part of me felt superior, and part of me felt the need to know something about these people from whom I was always kept apart.

'What's your name?' I asked, bouncing down to the bottom step. She looked at me with a mixture of suspicion and curiosity.

'Brigid,' she said hoarsely. 'My name is Brigid.'

'I'm Esty,' I said, when she didn't ask for mine. 'That's short for Esther. I live here.' I wanted her to think that I lived in the Big House.

She just nodded and continued to wrap her clothes around her purple-tinged legs. 'I could play with you, if you like,' I went on.

'I don't feel like it,' Brigid said. 'I'm waiting for me mam.'

She didn't ask me any questions. That disappointed me because I wanted her to think how fortunate she was that I was speaking to her and telling her all about my life. But then her mother came out with a jug of soup and led her away.

That night, I sought out my oldest hairbrush and put

it by for Brigid. Tomorrow I would give it to her, and that would be good. She would be happy and she'd play with me.

I waited eagerly until the ragged people shuffled up the avenue again. How pleased they would be that I had a present for Brigid! Yes, there she was, clinging to her mother. I waited until her mother sat her down on the Big House steps again and then I ran across the avenue with the hairbrush.

'Take it,' I said. 'It's for you. It's a present.' I wanted her to be grateful. I wanted her to look at me and make me feel good. But she merely looked at the hairbrush and didn't respond when I put it down beside her.

'We could play,' I said.

Brigid pulled those rags around her mottled legs.

'When someone gives you a nice present, the least you could do is look happy,' I said, trying to keep the annoyance out of my voice.

'Thanks, Miss,' she said. But she didn't clutch the hairbrush. She doesn't care, I thought. I've given her something and she doesn't care.

When her mother came to fetch her, she left the hairbrush on the step. I felt like running after her, but her mother might say something unpleasant, so I just watched them straggle away, the mother with her arm around the daughter.

Coaxing friendship from this ragged girl had become an obsession. Early the next morning, Mama said that the soup had gone off and that the ladies were adding more water to it.

'They've already watered it down,' she said. 'For the past two days they've been watering it down. It's useless stuff. It's gone beyond nourishment for those poor wretches, and still they keep coming.'

'What choice do they have?' Grandpa said. 'Where can they turn, Kate?'

Mama sighed. 'I'll take a few turnips and some bacon and slip them into the soup. Some of those ladies could well afford to bring a couple of bones to add nourishment,' she added bitterly. 'But they probably keep them for their dogs.'

Her words prompted me to sneak a slice of the smoked bacon into my pocket.

'Look, Brigid,' I said, when her mother left her on the step the next day. 'I've brought you some meat.'

She took the slice of smoked bacon from me and looked at it, as if she didn't know what to do with it.

'Eat it up,' I said. 'And then we can play.'

She took a bite, but it made her cough, and she spat it out.

I took her hand.

'Let's play.' I said. 'We can be friends.'

That's when she fell down.

'Come on, Brigid,' I cried. 'Get up and play with me.'

But she didn't get up. I tried to shake her – after all, her eyes were open and she must be able to see me. But still she didn't get up.

When her mother came, I told her that Brigid was awfully tired. Her mother dropped the jug of watery soup with a wail, and suddenly there were other people around, all wailing.

'It wasn't my fault,' I pleaded. 'I just wanted her to eat the food I gave her and play with me. But she wouldn't get up.'

By now, some of the high-born ladies had appeared, along with Mama, who drew me away.

'Shush, *alannah*,' she said. 'The poor girl is gone.'

'I gave her some bacon, Mama,' I cried. 'She just spat it out. Did I do wrong?'

Mama shook her head as she led me away.

'You didn't do wrong,' she said. 'The poor child was beyond saving.'

And that was my first experience of death. It was the moment when I really understood what was going on outside my cocooned life.

The diseased, exhausted land had nothing left to offer, and life there was hanging by an unravelling thread.

Chapter Two

It was shortly after the late-night whisperings became more intense that two gentlemen arrived in a carriage. I was puzzled as to why they'd come to our home rather than the Big House, but I said nothing because I was excited. Their rich clothes and air of confidence made a change from the destitute souls whose eyes I had avoided since the day Brigid fell down.

Mama's face was white and tense as she showed them into the parlour. And later, when raised voices came from that quarter, she clung to me so tightly, I couldn't breathe.

Grandpa was the first to emerge, shaking his head as he sank into his chair by the fire.

'He's sent his own men over,' he muttered at last. 'They won't listen to reason. Compassion? Pah!' he scoffed, spitting into the fire. 'They don't understand the word.'

Mama covered her face with her hands.

'Who?' I asked. 'What men? What are you talking about, Grandpa?'

Grandpa looked up at Mama, but she had turned away, her head bowed as she leaned on the window ledge.

'Nothing for you to worry about, Esty,' he said at last. 'Don't heed me, lass.'

'I'm not a baby,' I said. 'Yet nobody will tell me anything. Am I part of this family, or aren't I?'

Mama turned. I expected her to reprimand me for the outburst, but she looked at me as if seeing me in a new light.

'Yes, Esty,' she said quietly. 'You are part of the family, and you have seen things that no child your age should witness. And yes, you should know what's happening.' She held up her hand as Grandpa began to protest. 'Esty, you'll have to understand why these wretches have been calling at the door for Papa.'

'Really, Kate,' Grandpa interrupted. 'Is this necessary?'

I was scared by the way Mama's eyes focused unblinkingly on me. I backed away, suddenly not wanting to hear whatever she had to say.

'They keep calling here,' Mama went on, 'to plead for mercy because they have no money to pay their rent. Esty, do you know what happens to people who do not pay their rent?' I shook my head and wished she'd stop. 'They are evicted, child. The bailiffs put them out of their homes and then knock their miserable cottages to the ground.'

'Papa wouldn't do that,' I cried. 'Papa wouldn't allow anyone to do that.'

'Nor would he,' Grandpa put in. 'Your papa has been holding off the rent collections to give these people a chance, a hope that the land will soon be back to normal.

But Lord Craythorn has got wind of this, and has sent over two clerks to collect the rents. Their word is law – no rent means eviction.'

'But Papa…' I began.

Mama's lips hardened to a straight line. 'Papa will lose his position – and this house – if he doesn't comply with His Lordship's orders. He must put people out of their miserable cottages or else *we* will have to join the band of beggars. Now, Esty, do you understand?'

I ran from the room. I didn't want to understand. I just wanted everything to be as it had been before the potato blight.

Later on, Grandpa came and sat on my bed. 'Don't worry, Esty, lass,' he said, smoothing my hair from my face. 'Your papa will sort things out, you'll see. Your papa is strong and clever, he'll find a way.'

I knew from the way he said it that he was trying to comfort me. But I wanted so much to believe him, that I almost convinced myself he was right. Papa would find a way.

Two days later Mr and Mrs Reilly came to see Papa. I knew them. They used to come in the good days to pay their rent and bring me dollies and Saint Brigid's crosses made from rushes. Sometimes Mr Reilly let me drive the donkey and cart to the end of the avenue. Now their faces were thin and strained, just like the rest.

Mama showed them into the kitchen and gave them some goat's milk and corn bread. She tried to make conversation, but the old couple were too troubled to respond. Their faces lit up when Papa came in.

'Oh, Mr Maher,' said Mrs Reilly, rising up to clutch Papa's arm. 'They're coming. They've told us they're coming. We begged and begged, but...' she broke off and wrung her hands.

At that point, Mama sent me from the kitchen. I hung around outside the door for a while to try to make sense of the muffled voices. Then I decided that I didn't want to hear because I knew from the urgent tone that it was just more trouble. You never grow accustomed to the sound of trouble, it just grinds its way deeper into your mind each time, and you wonder how far it must grind before you have no mind left.

I ran through the yard, past the stables. I bit back tears of frustration as I kept on running, beyond the bridge end which marked the boundary of Lord Craythorn's estate. I stopped at the place where a cluster of small cottages had once stood. I often passed this way with Papa when we went to town to order supplies before one of His Lordship's infrequent visits to the estate. It used to make me laugh when the children from the cottages ran after the pony and trap. It made me feel like a real lady, looking down at the laughing, barefoot youngsters.

There was no laughing now. The cottages were either deserted or reduced to heaps of stone and thatch after the bailiffs' wrecking. It was as if everyone had been suddenly swallowed up. I was startled when a man shuffled out from behind one of the cottages. He was holding a cross made from two sticks. The skin on his face was yellowed and saggy, yet he seemed no older than Papa. We looked at one another for a moment.

Then he pointed to a small mound of earth beside the cabin.

'My wife,' he said. 'My wife.' He bent down and pushed the cross into the mound.

'Is she dead?' I asked, then bit my knuckles for asking such a stupid question.

The man nodded, as he stood upright again and looked at his handiwork. I didn't know what to do. If I ran away, it would seem rude. So I stood silently too.

'It's come to this,' he said eventually. 'We bury our dead where they die.' He gestured to the barren fields. 'All around us, the graves of good people scattered in a dead land. Starved men, women and babes, buried where they fall.'

Then he stared at me. 'Where are you going, child?' he asked, as if he was suddenly aware of my presence. 'Why are you not with your people? Have they died? You can't stay here alone. You must find help. You must go to the workhouse.'

I didn't know what to say. As he looked at me, I was conscious of my shoes and my warm clothes.

'Are you from the estate?' he asked.

I swallowed. I no longer wished to be seen as a privileged lady. I belonged nowhere, and I was feeling guilty just for being alive.

'Are you from the estate?' he asked again.

I nodded, and tried to say I was from the Craythorn estate where my Papa was trying to prevent evictions. But the words wouldn't come, because of the anger in his voice.

He shook his head slowly and spat on the road, just as Grandpa did when he was angered by people's words or actions.

I watched him for a moment, shuffling down the road, his ragged coat flapping. The cross he'd put on his wife's grave fell over, and I knew it was because he hadn't had the strength to push it down far enough into the hard ground.

I didn't touch it, but turned for home.

Chapter Three

I was glad to see that the Reillys had left. I didn't want to see their troubled faces, knowing I couldn't help.

Mama was in the kitchen. It was warm and comforting and I wished we could just close the door and shut out all the misery – Papa, Mama, Grandpa and me.

I could hear Grandpa coughing in his room at the back. That meant he was reading. He always smoked his pipe when he was reading. Grandpa had once been a teacher. His small school had closed when families moved away to bigger towns in search of work.

I shared his love of books. 'Knowledge is the greatest weapon against life's kicks and barbs,' he often said. But all the knowledge in the world couldn't deal with what was happening to us in Ireland.

'Where's Papa?' I asked.

Mama looked up from the turnip she was peeling. Grandpa had buried the turnip crop under rushes and straw to preserve them, but they were starting to rot, just like everything else around here.

'He's gone to the Big House,' Mama sighed, paring away some black turnip peel.

'With those men?'

She nodded, her lips pressed together in that line that always made me fearful.

'Will he be all right?' I asked. 'I wish they'd go away, Mama. They scare me.'

Mama put the clean part of the turnip into a basin of cold water, then dried her hands in her apron.

'They scare all of us, Esty,' she said. 'But there's nothing we can do. Papa is trying to make them see reason. He's taken them to see for themselves the state of the small farms around, to make them understand why the tenants can't pay their rent.'

Lucky that I didn't meet them on the road, I thought. Papa would not have been pleased.

'Will we have to go to the workhouse?' I asked Mama, as I gathered up the peelings and dumped them into a bucket.

Mama looked up sharply. 'What are you talking about, Esty?'

I shrugged my shoulders. 'I heard that it's a place where people go who have no homes. Will we have to go there if Papa doesn't get the rents? You said we'd be beggars if…'

'Don't talk like that,' Mama scolded. 'I don't want to hear that sort of talk.'

'Is it a bad place, the workhouse?' I persisted.

Mama shook her head. 'They say the rules are terrible and people lose all their dignity. They have nothing left when they get that far, Esty. No homes, no money, families divided up. It's bad to have to depend on the charity of others for your very existence.'

I wished I could tell her about the man I'd met. Tell her about his dead wife in a hole in the ground outside his cottage, and the cross that fell down when he went away. But I could see that Mama was tired.

When Papa came home later, he was troubled. He sat silently gazing into the flames that flickered between the bars of the range. Mama didn't ask any questions, and we ate in silence.

I didn't sleep that night. I could hear subdued murmurings from the kitchen and I knew that whatever had happened between Papa and those men was being discussed. When you have only hints, denials and half-knowledge, your imagination wraps them into a gigantic trouble that fevers your sleepless mind. Not knowing is far more frightening than knowing.

So I was wide awake when I heard voices early next morning, just before daybreak. Papa? I ran downstairs in my nightdress.

Mama, white-faced and pleading, was trying to prevent Papa from leaving.

'What can you do?' she cried. 'You can't stand up to their might...' She broke off when she saw me on the stairs. 'Go back to bed, Esty,' she said.

'Papa?' I ran to my father. 'Where are you going, Papa?'

He smiled, and lifted me up. 'I'll be back for breakfast,' he said. 'You be a good girl.' Then he whispered in my ear, 'You're my strong sweetheart, Esty. You look after Mama for me – all right?'

I smiled. He was treating me like a grown-up,

even if it was with words that had no meaning. Mama was Mama; she didn't need looking after. I hugged him. His beard tickled my face and his tweed coat felt rough as he let me down.

Those are the last memories I have of Papa.

Chapter Four

A loud knocking on the door came later in the morning. Mama dropped the jug she'd just filled from the bucket of goat's milk. Grandpa held out his hand to stop her going to the door and opened it himself.

Mama sank into a chair. What was she afraid of? Her terrified eyes were fixed on the door.

There were several voices. Then Grandpa came back indoors. His face was ashen. Mama looked at him in silence. I wanted to scream. Something was happening. Something bad.

'Kate,' he said.

Mama hid her face in her apron. 'No!' she cried. 'No!'

I was too frightened to ask what had happened. A cold fear took hold of me. Something had happened that would change our lives – I knew that.

Some men came in. I recognised them as tenants who used to come and pay their rent to Papa. They stood awkwardly in front of Mama. She looked at them and shook her head.

'I told him,' she said. 'I told him he couldn't take on the might of those…' Her voice tapered off in a sob.

'He tried, Missus,' said one of the men, twisting his cap nervously in his hands. 'He tried talking to them, but they just pushed him away. Then we all tried to stop them.' He shrugged.

'He fought bravely,' the other man put in. 'But Lord Craythorn's bailiffs were just too strong. Troops, Missus. They had troops with them. They don't know how things are here. They treated us like criminals. Your husband tried to reason with them, make them understand. But they just got the battering ram and when he stood in their path to stop them, they didn't stop.'

Mama suddenly became composed. She took a deep breath.

'Where is he?' she said evenly. 'Where is my husband?'

'Outside,' one of the men said.

'Well, bring him in. We'll give him a proper wake.'

Wake?

'No!' I screamed. 'No! Papa's not dead!'

Grandpa held me while the rest of the men carried in Papa's body on the door of the very house – the Reillys' house – that he'd been trying to protect. I bit into my fist. That broken creature laid out on a crude door could not be my Papa!

But the truth was there. Papa was gone.

A few weeks later, I was dusting the sideboard. Doing something familiar can help restore sense to life –

that's what Mama said. The mirror had no magic now. All I could see was my own white face and sunken eyes.

I'd been used to callers coming to weep with Mama, so I was only mildly curious when a carriage drew up outside. The parlour door opened, and a rustle of silk announced a woman whom I recognised as one of the high-born ladies who had shooed me out of the Big House kitchen. She looked at me and gave a slight nod.

'What a beautiful sideboard,' she said, running her finger over the polished surface. I automatically wiped the place she had touched, as Mama showed her to the best armchair. Mama looked at me and smiled. But it wasn't a real smile, it was a mouth smile which had no meaning because her eyes were so anxious.

'Esty,' she said. 'Mrs Burgess has come to talk. Will you put on the kettle for some tea?'

I hopped down from the chair, glad to get away from this haughty lady who seemed all wrong in our parlour. Grandpa was sitting by the range, wiping the eggs he'd collected.

'There's a lady with Mama,' I said to him. 'Mrs Burgess – one of the soup ladies.'

Grandpa sniffed, and continued wiping the eggs.

'Something to do with the soup, maybe?' I said, and swallowed hard. 'Or could it be to put us out of our house?' From half-heard conversations I was aware that, with Papa gone, we were no longer entitled to live in the middleman's house.

Grandpa stopped what he was doing and looked at me sharply. 'No, lass. She can't do that. The Burgesses own the mill. She's probably here to sympathise. Best put on that kettle you're holding. It won't boil by itself.'

He put the bowl of eggs down carefully on the dresser – precious eggs – because we only had three laying hens left. Grandpa had given the rest to some of the destitute callers, including the evicted Reillys who'd gone to live with their son. Grandpa said that they'd get a better welcome if they had a couple of hens to take with them.

When Mama came to make the tea, I helped her set the tray with the best china that my grandma had left her, along with the sideboard. They had been Grandma's wedding presents from the Earl of Kildare. Mama often told me what a fine person Grandma had been.

'She was educated,' Mama used to say proudly. 'When she worked as a nursemaid for the Earl, the children's governess became her friend and taught her to read and write. She passed that on to me.'

'And you passed it on to me,' I'd laugh. 'You and Grandpa.'

'Come with me,' she said, when the tray was set. 'Come and talk to Mrs Burgess, Esty.'

'No, Mama,' I replied. 'I wouldn't know what to say to her.'

'Do come,' Mama said. 'It's courteous, Esty, to talk to visitors.'

'Please, Mama. I'd rather not.'

'I insist,' Mama said sharply.

Grandpa looked at her, but said nothing.

I frowned, and muttered, 'All right. But please

don't make me stay for long, Mama.'

I followed her reluctantly out of the kitchen, glancing back at Grandpa. He shrugged his shoulders and smiled encouragingly.

Mrs Burgess looked me up and down when I entered the room. I hoped that my shoes were clean and my stockings were smooth.

'So you're Esther,' she said.

'Yes, Ma'am,' I said with a curtsy, because Mama said that's what you did in the presence of high-born people.

'Come over here, child, and let me look at you.'

I looked at Mama, who nodded, and I went towards the lace-gloved hand that stretched out to me. Even through the lace I could feel the coldness of the hand that took mine. I wished she'd let me go.

'Your mama tells me you can read and write, dear. Is that so?'

'Yes, Ma'am,' I replied. 'My mama taught me.'

'Well, well,' Mrs Burgess chuckled. 'Aren't you the lucky one, Esther. Not many children of middlemen have such good fortune, you know.'

At the mention of my father, I wanted to rip my hand away and run from this haughty woman who was making me nervous just by looking at me. But Mama would be horrified.

Mama poured tea and handed it to Mrs Burgess.

Mrs Burgess continued to look at me as she sipped her tea.

'Are you a strong girl, dear?' she asked. 'You look rather small for your age.'

'Oh, indeed she is, Madam,' Mama said eagerly. 'Esther is a very strong girl. She does all sorts of work, don't you, Esther?'

I gave Mama a puzzled look, and nodded.

'Run along, child,' Mrs Burgess said eventually.

I gave a great sigh of relief and, with another half-curtsy, left them to talk.

Grandpa was sitting at the range, deep in the thoughts that had preoccupied him since Papa's death. Deep, sad thoughts just like Mama's and mine, except that he kept them locked inside, while Mama and I wept away ours.

'Thank goodness that's over,' I said, sitting on the arm of his chair. 'I don't like that woman, Grandpa. She makes me nervous.'

'Me too, lass,' he said. 'Full of nonsense. The type who'd like us all to lick her boots, eh?'

'Not me,' I laughed.

'Me neither,' he laughed.

When we heard the front door close, and the crunch of the carriage wheels on the avenue, Grandpa winked at me. 'She's flown back to her lair,' he said.

We both looked up expectantly when Mama came back into the kitchen, carrying the tray. She said nothing as she moved the china on to the table. Then she wiped the tray and put it on the dresser.

'Well?' Grandpa said eventually. 'What did the grand Mrs Burgess have to say?'

Mama came over and took my two hands in hers.

'Esty,' she said, looking into my eyes. 'Mrs Burgess is taking you on.'

'What!' Grandpa exclaimed, jumping up from his chair.

'What do you mean, Mama?' I cried.

'Oh, Kate,' Grandpa said, putting his hand on my shoulder. 'Esty's so young.'

Mama hung her head for a moment, then looked up at me. 'It's for the best, Esty,' she said. 'We have to leave this house soon. You'll have a good home and learn to be a lady's maid. Mrs Burgess has promised that you will be well looked after. A lady's maid, Esty! Just think: in a few years you could be in London, Paris even, as personal maid to some high-born lady!'

'I don't want to be a lady's maid,' I protested. 'I want to stay here with you and Grandpa. Don't send me away, Mama. Please.'

I ran to Grandpa and he held me close. 'Listen to your mama,' he said.

Mama slowly shook her head. 'We have no choice, Esty,' she said tearfully. 'Very soon we'll have to find a cottage somewhere. At least I'll know that you are being looked after, that you'll be spared all that. Don't you see, dearest? We have no choice.'

Grandpa sat down again and hung his head.

'So it's come to this,' he murmured.

Chapter Five

When Mrs Burgess's pony and trap came to collect me three days later, Grandpa didn't come to the door to see me off. I knew he was in his room, and Mama said it was best to leave him be.

It was just as well. I was trying so hard to be brave. I knew that if Grandpa was there, I'd let go of all the frightened, frustrated screams that were in my chest.

Mama held me very close as the Burgess's groom lifted my bag into the trap.

'You'll be well looked after, Esty,' she said, brushing a stray lock of hair from my face. 'Just think' – her voice took on a forced note of jollity – 'you'll be the baby of the staff and everyone will want to mother you.'

I just want *you* to mother me, I thought. But that would upset her.

'Don't look back, Esty,' she said as she helped me into the trap, 'It's easier if you don't.'

I nodded, fighting back my tears.

With a 'Hup!' from the groom, and a crack of the whip, the trap moved off. I bit my lip to stop myself from crying out.

I looked at the groom. He was young, about nineteen,

and had a strong face. Perhaps he'd be nice to me. I would talk to him on the journey and he might watch out for me at the Burgess estate.

When we reached the end of the avenue, I looked back. Grandpa had come out and was standing with his arm around Mama. Her head was on his shoulder, her hands over her face, just like the day we'd buried Papa.

'Grandpa!' I shouted, jumping up. 'Grandpa, I can't do this!'

He began to run down the avenue, waving his hand.

'Sit down, Missy,' the groom snapped. 'I can't control the trap if you're jumping about.'

His manner scared me. I took one last look back. Grandpa was standing in the middle of the avenue with a lost look on his face. He raised his hand and gave a feeble wave. I didn't wave back.

The groom looked at me as the horse settled into a trot on the empty road.

'Are you going into service?' he asked.

I nodded, trying not to burst into tears.

'You're a bit young, ain't you?' he went on. 'What are you, nine?'

I wiped my nose and took a deep breath. 'I'm nearly thirteen,' I said.

'Ha!' he laughed, tapping the horse with the whip. 'Taking on children now, are they? You won't last long, Missy. You couldn't even reach the sink.'

'I'm to be trained as a lady's maid,' I said. 'Lady's maids have nothing to do with sinks.'

He laughed again. 'You'll find out soon enough.'

The five miles to the Burgess estate seemed to go on for ever. Every turn of the wheels was taking me farther from home. Then I reminded myself that, in a few days' time, the house I'd grown up in would no longer be my home.

After a long silence, the groom asked, 'What's your name?'

'What?' I looked up.

'Your name. You do have a name, don't you?'

'Esty,' I said. 'Esty Maher. What's yours?'

'John Joe,' he replied, tapping the horse with the whip again. 'That's me.' Then he looked straight at me. 'Your *da*, was he the Craythorn middleman?' I nodded, waiting for him to spit. I knew by now that many middlemen were not as honest or trustworthy as Papa.

'Brave man,' John Joe went on, looking at the road again. 'Good that someone stands up for the poor.'

I felt relieved and comforted. For the rest of the journey we talked, only lapsing into silence when we passed tattered people grouped around a demolished cottage or a crude grave. Once I nearly screamed when I saw a man pull an old lady up out of a hole in the boggy land beyond the roadside.

'*Scalpeens*,' John Joe muttered.

'What's that?'

'*Scalpeens*,' he repeated. 'They're holes and trenches in the ground that evicted people dig out for shelter. They're allowed to take part of the thatch from their broken home and use it to make a shelter on common land.'

'Oh, no!' I exclaimed. 'That's awful.'

John Joe shrugged. 'Happening everywhere,' he said. 'We're lucky, Esty. Work is hard at the Burgess estate. At least we have food and lodging.'

But all I could think was: *would this be the fate of Grandpa and Mama?*

I voiced my fear to John Joe. He shook his head.

'No,' he said. 'Your *da* was a middleman. There'll be money. There'll be good things to sell and there'll be some of your father's wages due. Your family can afford to rent a cottage on the estate – you'll see.'

As we passed through the back gates of the Burgess estate, I thought I was going to be sick.

John Joe grinned at me as he reined in the horse in the courtyard beside the stables.

'Home, my lady,' he said, sweeping an exaggerated bow and helping me down from the trap.

Chapter Six

I stood awkwardly at the kitchen door when John Joe tried to usher me through. Although the kitchen wasn't as big as Lord Craythorn's, it was much busier, with more servants. But then, I'd never been allowed into the Big House when his lordship was in residence, so, apart from the soup days, I was unused to such kitchen bustle. I clutched my bag and hoped nobody would see me. However, everyone was too busy to notice.

John Joe pulled me towards the stout back of a lady who was standing at the huge iron range, where pots steamed and bubbled with frightening intensity.

'Mrs Casey!' John Joe shouted over the din. 'Mrs Casey!'

'What?' she said, turning around impatiently. I shrank closer to John Joe when I saw her red, steam-hot face frowning at being disturbed. But the frown disappeared when she saw John Joe.

'Ah, it's yourself, lad,' she said. Then she noticed me trying to hide behind him. 'And who have you got there, eh?'

John Joe pushed me in front of him. I kept my eyes firmly on the floor, wishing I could slip between the flagstones.

'Miss Esty Maher,' said John Joe with a laugh. 'At your service. Go on, Miss Esty, say hello to Mrs Casey, mistress of this kitchen and a woman to be feared by all and sundry – even them upstairs.'

Mrs Casey laughed and offered me a plump hand. 'Come here, *alannah,* and let's have a look at you. My, you are a tiny little thing, aren't you, eh?'

'Going to be a lady's maid,' John Joe went on. 'Isn't that right, Esty? None of your kitchen antics for her, Mrs Casey. She's going places, is Esty.'

I wished he'd stop. I was conscious of other eyes on me as staff walked past.

'Well, is that a fact, now?' chuckled Mrs Casey. 'We'll have to put some flesh on those bones then, won't we?' Then her tone became serious. 'We were all sorry to hear about your papa, *alannah*,' she went on. 'A brave middleman. Stood up for the poor tenants. Not like some.'

When I looked up at her soft, kindly face, I wanted to clutch her apron and beg her to ask Mrs Burgess to let me go home.

There was a sudden lessening of chatter. Mrs Casey stood upright, her hands on her hips. 'Hm,' she sniffed.

'What's going on here?' a crisp voice asked. 'John Joe, you shouldn't be here. Go at once to your stable duties. Mrs Casey, how is lunch progressing? Mrs Burgess has some pressing engagements in the afternoon.'

Then: 'Who is this child, and what is she doing here?'

I shrank away from the thin, black clad woman, her sharp features emphasised by grey hair caught back in a tight bun at the nape of her wrinkled neck.

'Miss Esty Maher,' said Mrs Casey, pushing me in front of her. 'I'm surprised you don't know about her,' she added with an air of triumph. 'After all, Mrs Burgess particularly asked for her to come into service here.'

'This girl?' The lady was slightly taken aback as she peered at me. 'This is the new…?' But she quickly regained her composure. 'What are you doing here in the kitchen?' she said to me.

I didn't know how to answer. I was close to tears. But Mrs Casey answered for me. 'John Joe went and fetched her, Miss Burke,' she said. 'The child has just arrived.'

'He should not have brought her to the kitchen,' snapped Miss Burke. 'She's expected upstairs. John Joe should have known.'

'Perhaps nobody told him,' Mrs Casey said with a sniff, before turning back to her pots on the range.

Miss Burke poked me in the shoulder. 'Take your bag and follow me,' she said, striding away. I looked at Mrs Casey for a comforting glance, but she was busily stirring something in one of the big saucepans. I ran to catch up with Miss Burke, and this time I could see the curious faces turned in my direction. I followed Miss Burke up what I would soon come to know as the staff stairs.

When we reached the front hall, she looked me up and down. I automatically rubbed each shoe on the back of my legs and brushed down my coat.

'Wait there,' she said, then knocked at a white, panelled door.

When she was summoned inside, my eyes took in the huge hall. A big table with a vase of flowers took up the centre of the hall. The tiled floor was scattered with richly patterned rugs. Paintings hung along the walls and above them were exotic animals' heads mounted on wood, some of them snarling with sharp teeth as though they were still fighting against their captivity. I gazed up at the glassy-eyed creatures and wondered what misfortune had brought them to gather dust in a house in Ireland.

'Come along, child. Don't dawdle. And leave that bag there.'

I jumped. Then I took a deep breath and went to meet my employer.

Mrs Burgess was sitting on a sofa before a large fire, a small glass in her hand. A girl of about sixteen sat opposite, her green silk dress fastened at the neck with tiny buttons. Behind her, a young woman in a starchy white apron was pouring something from a jug. Miss Burke nudged me ahead of her, before withdrawing and closing the door.

Now I was alone before these strangers. I just wanted to turn and flee.

'Come over here, child,' said Mrs Burgess, holding out her hand. The standing woman looked at me with curiosity.

'This is Esther,' Mrs Burgess went on. I wasn't asked to sit, so I just stood there, unsure of what to do with my hands. 'The child I told you about, May,' she said, looking at the other woman who was handing a glass of juice to the girl in the green dress. 'May is lady's maid to my daughter, Miss Emma,' Mrs Burgess said to me. 'She'll be teaching you all you need to know. You'll be sharing a room with May and you'll have your meals below stairs.' She paused.

I didn't know if I should speak or not, so I just stood awkwardly in silence.

Miss Emma looked at me as she took a sip of juice. I licked my lips, partly from nervousness and partly because I'd had nothing to eat or drink since the evening before.

'She's very young, Mama,' she said. 'I can't think why we want another lady's maid. May does well enough for me.'

'Shush, Emma,' replied her mother. 'This is an act of charity. Esther's father was middleman for Lord Craythorn. He died, dear.'

'Lord Craythorn?' exclaimed Miss Emma. 'Has he died?'

'No, of course not. His middleman has died.'

'Oh,' said Miss Emma. I couldn't but note her relief that it was my papa who had died, and not Lord Craythorn. I wished they would all die right there, with their drinks and silk dresses. I was a mere act of charity. How I longed for Mama and Grandpa.

Mrs Burgess and her daughter continued to chat as if I wasn't there until, as if brushing away a bothersome fly, Mrs Burgess turned towards me.

'You may go now, Esther. May will tend to you later.'

I swallowed hard. 'Where shall I go, Ma'am?'

Miss Emma laughed. 'Downstairs, girl. Where do you think?'

'No, dear,' put in her mother. 'May can take her. Besides, it's almost lunchtime, so May will be leaving anyway.'

I was so glad to get away that I forgot to curtsy. May caught my arm before I reached the door.

'Don't ever do that again,' she said, indicating the two ladies. 'You must always remember to take your leave of gentry in a proper manner. You're part of this household and you must act properly.'

'Yes, Miss,' I muttered miserably, turning to curtsy.

'Well done, May,' said Mrs Burgess. 'I can see you'll knock the rough corners off the girl.'

May's words stuck in my mind as I followed her.

Part of this household? Never.

Chapter Seven

'I hope you don't snore,' May said, as I unpacked my things into the chest of drawers beside the iron bedstead she'd pointed me towards.

'I don't think so,' I replied nervously.

Our small room was at the top of the house. It had a slanted ceiling with a window that looked straight up into the sky. The wooden floor was scattered with colourful rag rugs, which added a comforting note to the austere furniture – a large wardrobe, a washstand and a ladder-back chair with clothes folded on it. There was a bookshelf too, but no books.

'I made those,' May remarked, nodding towards the rugs. 'Made them from bits of fabric left over from Miss Emma's dressmaker.'

'They're beautiful,' I said.

'Yes, well, you take care you don't walk on them, Missy.' She removed her white apron and folded it on her bed.

Don't snore and don't walk on the floor. Could it get any worse? 'I'm sorry, Miss,' I said.

May looked at me. 'Pardon?' she said. 'Sorry for what?'

'That you have to share your room with me. I know you don't want to, but it's not my fault.'

To my surprise, May laughed, which made her look much younger than I'd thought. She couldn't have been more than eighteen. 'Stop looking so miserable, Esther. I'm joking. Can't you tell when someone is joking?'

I shrugged. 'Not really,' I replied.

'Well you'd better get used to it, dear. It's the only thing that'll keep you sane in this madhouse. Besides, I'm pleased to have company. It'll be nice to have someone to talk to up here.'

'Really?' I said, brightening up.

'Yes, really. What do you think it's like having to bow and scrape to Miss Emma all day, every day? "May, do this. May, fetch me that." Sometimes I want to scream and pull her hair.'

She stopped, and laughed. 'Picture that if you can.' Then she frowned and leaned towards me. 'I hope you won't repeat what I've just said. I'd lose my job. Me and my mouth! My mother, God rest her, always said it would get me into trouble.'

'Of course I won't say anything,' I assured her. 'I'm not a telltale.'

'Good. We can chat here, Esther. But outside this door it will be different, you understand? I have my position, you have yours. My job, I've been told, is to train you to be a lady's maid. I'll pull you up, just like I did as we left the parlour. That will keep the ladies happy and make me look good. Then you'll probably be passed on to some other household.'

'What?' I exclaimed.

'Oh, don't worry. That won't be for ages. Just realise that, while you're training, you will be given other duties as well. You'll have to earn your keep. Now, smarten up, we're going down to lunch. I hope they'll let you sit with me.'

'What do you mean, *let* me sit with you?' I asked.

'Household hierarchy,' laughed May. 'Everyone has their own place at table, according to their rank. Mr Egan, the butler sits at the top with Miss Burke. Then come the rest of us; me, housemaids, coachman, right down to the stable lads and scullery maids who sit at the bottom.'

'Where do you sit?' I asked.

'Towards the top,' May said with a smile. 'Which is why I don't have many friends among the staff. Too low for the high, and too high for the low, if you get my meaning. Now, hurry, Esther. There'll be a fuss if we're late.'

'Esty,' I said. 'Call me Esty.'

The kitchen was hot and steamy and filled with chatter as the staff took their places on either side of the long table. May gave me a sympathetic look when I was directed to sit at the bottom of the table. I was conscious of the curious, cold stares from the two scullery maids as I sat down to share their bench. I looked around for John Joe, but there was no sign of him. I wondered if he lived with his family outside the estate, and hoped not. I needed friends here at this hostile end of the table. I stood up with the others as the butler solemnly said grace. Then the chatter started up again.

One of the scullery maids leaned towards me.

'I know you,' she said. 'I seen you with your *da*, in your pony and trap.'

'Have you?' I said.

'Yes. All la-di-da, thinking you were better than the rest of us. We used to run after you, me and me brother, hoping you'd throw us a coin or two. But you never did. You're not so la-di-da now, are you, Miss Snooty?'

I blushed with embarrassment. The scullery maid sniggered as she helped herself from the stew-pot that filtered down from the other end of the table. By the time the pot got to me, there was very little left. As I tried to scoop out the sticky remains, the two maids giggled.

There was a draught when the back door opened. John Joe! I breathed a sigh of relief at the sight of his familiar face.

'You're late, boy,' Mr Egan said with a scowl.

'Sorry, sir,' said John Joe, pulling out a chair opposite me. 'Horse had a stone in her hoof.'

'Well, you must suffer the consequences,' the butler said grandly. 'We have all had our share.'

'It's all right,' put in Mrs Casey, getting up from the table and going to the range. 'I knew the lad was delayed, so I've saved him some stew.'

He winked at her cheekily as she put a fresh plate before him. Then he spotted me.

'Well, Miss Esther Maher,' he said with a laugh. 'How are they treating you?'

I blushed again, and concentrated on the sticky mess on my plate.

'Not very well,' giggled the first scullery maid. 'The mighty Miss Maher has to take her place with us now. A pot-scrubber, just like me and Rose.'

'Watch your tongue, Betty Murphy,' said John Joe. 'Esty's had to put up with just as much as the rest of us. You and your family have done well from the Burgess table, so consider yourself lucky.'

'Well, her da's a middleman,' retorted Betty Murphy. 'No fear of them goin' hungry.'

'Esty's *da* died trying to stop the bailiffs,' said John Joe. 'So let that be enough from you.'

I blushed, wishing I could just disappear under the table. It was then I noticed the other scullery maid slipping bits of her stew and bread into a cloth spread on her lap. She looked at me with a mixture of guilt and fear. I looked away quickly. Whatever she was up to, it was none of my business.

When at last the meal was over, everyone dispersed. I made to move away with May when I saw Miss Burke coming towards me.

'Wait, young woman,' she said. 'Your duties are here in the kitchen.'

I started to stutter that I was training to be a lady's maid, but she cut me short.

'Training, yes,' she said. 'But don't you know that training comes at a price? Your training is confined to afternoons only. Other than that, your place is with the other servants. Now, start clearing up with Betty and Rose.'

I looked appealingly at May, but she just gave me

a helpless glance before leaving the kitchen. I looked at the huge amount of dishes and wondered where to begin.

'You can start by taking all those plates to the sink,' said Betty, with a smirk.

John Joe winked at me as he opened the back door.

'Don't let them get to you, Esty,' he said. 'You stand up to them.'

He was right. All the recent troubles in my life seemed to harden into an angry ball inside my head. It was time to grit my teeth and do as John Joe said.

'Fine,' I said, rolling up my sleeves. 'I can do that.' And, to my surprise, I felt my cringing attitude diminish.

Soon, the two scullery maids and I were the only ones left in the kitchen. Rose and I, with coarse aprons wrapped around us, were elbow-deep at the double sink, the gritty soap slipping in and out of my hands as I scrubbed.

'Thanks for sayin' nothin',' Rose whispered.

'What do you mean?' I asked.

'For sayin' nothin' about me savin' the bit of stew.'

'Why would I say anything?' I asked.

'Because it's forbidden,' replied Betty, scraping plates into a bucket. 'We're supposed to only feed ourselves. There's a back door collection for our families and the poor every morning. Mrs Burgess insists that she wants no sickly staff.'

'But if there's food collected for your family, then why are you giving away your dinner, Rose?'

'For her brother,' put in Betty as she lowered the scraped plates into the sink. 'He's on the run.'

'Shush, Betty Murphy,' hissed Rose, looking around. 'That's a secret.'

'On the run from what?' I asked, ignoring the smirking Betty. But neither of them replied.

Chapter Eight

In the weeks that followed, John Joe's words: *Stand up to them,* became my strength. My mornings began at six o'clock, heating water to take upstairs for Mrs Burgess and her daughter's wash-basins. The rest of the morning was spent mostly in the kitchen, scrubbing and cleaning or helping Mrs Casey prepare meals. By now, I had a uniform of a blue dress with puffed sleeves and a white apron for my afternoons with May. I also had to wear a starched bonnet which made my head itch. I learned how to wash and iron the Burgess women's clothes, how to mend tears and sew on buttons. The sewing was the best part, because May and I could chat as we sewed. That, and being with Mrs Casey made up for many of the other hardships.

'My mama is a very good cook,' I said when I was first assigned to Mrs Casey.

'Of course she is, *alannah*,' Mrs Casey chuckled. 'But your mama never had to cater for the likes of them upstairs. So, being a trainee lady's maid, you'll need to know how to make dainties.'

'All this doesn't seem right,' I said to her once.

'What are you saying, child?' she wheezed. 'Are you

saying my cooking is not up to quality?'

'No,' I replied. 'It's just that it doesn't seem right that we're here making pretty food and out there...' I nodded towards the window.

'The Hunger, is it?' Mrs Casey said, shaking her head as she spooned the mixture into baking tins. 'It's true, *alannah*. Don't think we don't feel it. We'll carry the guilt of surviving this for years, but what else can we do? Madam gives to as many as she can. You've seen them every morning at the back door. We give them what's left.'

'But it's not enough, is it, Mrs Casey? I wish we could do more.'

'None of our business,' she said. 'Some things are out of our control. We just have to thank God that we have good jobs and comfort. Now, don't you be going on too much about them out there. That will make people angry.'

So I kept my opinions to myself. My main worry was that Mama and Grandpa had enough to eat. When John Joe told me that Grandpa had got a job as a gardener on Lord Craythorn's estate, I was appalled.

'My grandpa is a middleman's father,' I protested. 'He was a schoolteacher. He shouldn't be doing menial...' I stopped when I saw John Joe shaking his head.

'No work is menial these days,' he said. 'Even though he's probably earning just a few shillings, if it helps pay the rent for the cottage they're in, then that's the most important thing. There's many would be happy to have that job. He only got it because of your father.'

He went on, 'I like your grandfather a lot. He's clever.'

I assumed John Joe was simply trying to humour me. I'd never thought of Grandpa in that light. To me, he was always just Grandpa.

I bit my lip and said no more. At least it was comforting to know that they weren't depending on my skimpy pay. Whenever he could, after delivering the master to the mill, John Joe would take the longer route by the Craythorn estate and deliver my notes and money to Mama. I kept Mama's replies under my pillow and kissed them each night – though I sometimes wondered why she never thanked me for the money.

Mrs Casey had tut-tutted when I first counted out my paltry allowance.

'There's nothing you can do, *alannah*,' she sympathised. 'We can't stand up against the gentry. They have the training of you, so I suppose they're entitled to keep back money for that.'

'But I work so hard, Mrs Casey,' I protested. 'Look at my red hands! I more than pay for my keep. It just doesn't seem fair. Rose and Betty get more than I do.'

'I know, child,' Mrs Casey said soothingly. 'But in time you'll be a true lady's maid and much better off.'

'I can't wait that long,' I muttered. 'Besides, I never wanted to be a lady's maid. It's pointless.'

Mrs Casey pretended to be shocked, and then chuckled. 'And what would you be, then, Esty?'

'I don't know,' I admitted. 'Something better. Something where I could use my mind.'

Mrs Casey's chuckle became a laugh. 'Mind?'

she said. 'Your mind won't put bread on the table, *alannah*.' She held up her hands. 'These,' she went on, 'these are what you need to stay alive. Working hands.'

'I'm not afraid of work,' I replied. 'It's just that I'd like to use my mind as well.'

Mrs Casey simply shook her head. 'There's a lot of hardship out there,' she said. 'There's no place for the likes of us to be using brains. Who would listen?'

Who indeed? I wanted to tell Mrs Casey that I'd seen a girl die in front of me. *Brigid* – her name still filled me with a cold chill. A small life, one of thousands, wiped out because nobody would listen to people like Papa. But I said nothing. Brigid was in a part of my mind that would always serve to remind me how fragile life is.

I noticed that Miss Emma discarded *The Illustrated London News* after she'd finished reading about the Paris fashions. I took to stuffing them under my apron and taking them to the room I shared with May.

'What are you doing with Miss Emma's magazine?' May said, her face aghast. 'There'll be trouble...'

'I don't think so,' I replied. 'I've been watching. As soon as she's read about the fashions she puts the magazine in the wastepaper basket. And she only gets a chance to read it when Sir and Madam have finished with it, so nobody wants it after that.'

'And what are you going to do with it?' asked May.

'Why, read it of course. What did you think?'

'You can read, Esty?' she exclaimed.

'Of course. Can't you, May?'

May shook her head. 'Never got the chance,' she muttered.

'I could teach you, if you like,' I offered.

'Could you?'

'Yes. We could save all these magazines and go through them together.'

'Goodness!' laughed May. 'That would be fun. Me reading!'

And so we kept our eyes open for discarded copies of *The Illustrated London News*. We also gathered candle stumps and melted them together to make up a full-size light. We looked forward to our nights together, sitting on May's bed with our quilts around us, peering at the small print as I taught May her letters.

'Best not say anything to the others, Esty,' she said. 'Them upstairs don't care for their lower staff to know their letters.' She added, with a laugh, 'Something to do with us getting above ourselves. And them downstairs would be jealous.'

'Mrs Burgess knows I can read and write,' I said.

'Maybe,' replied May. 'But she wouldn't boast about it.'

Somehow, the thoughts of those nights spent with May made each day's hardships easier to bear. I still fretted for Mama and Grandpa, but I got some comfort from knowing that the money I sent them would help in a small way, to keep them safe from hunger and eviction.

One night, while May was writing words into an old copybook I'd taken from the Burgess's now-disused schoolroom, an article about Ireland in *The Illustrated London News* caught my eye.

'May,' I said. 'Do you know what Whiteboys are? It says here that they are causing a lot of trouble…' I broke off as May looked at me with alarm.

'Whiteboys!' she said in a subdued voice. 'You must never mention that name here.'

'But who are they? They sound like a band of ruffians.'

'Rebels,' whispered May. 'They're a secret society – some of them decent, some of them bad – who fight against the crippling rents and the evictions. The decent ones steal a sheep or a pig from the landlord gentry and share out the meat. If they're caught…' May paused, '…if they're caught, they're either hanged or else transported to Australia, never to see their families again.'

'How do you know all this?' I asked.

May just shook her head. 'Just don't mention the word, Esty. Put Whiteboys right out of your head.'

'Do you know of any rebels around here?' I went on.

May said nothing. She pursed her lips and concentrated on a piece of torn lace on Miss Emma's petticoat.

'It's Rose, isn't it?' I whispered. 'Her brother…'

'Sshh,' hissed May. 'Don't mention names.'

'He's on the run, isn't he? I heard Betty say so.'

'Betty!' May hissed again. 'She's a big mouth.'

'It's true, then, isn't it?' I persisted. 'Rose's brother is one of those.' I pointed to the article I'd been reading.

'He's a good lad,' said May. 'He was almost caught stealing from Major Fawcett's kitchen. One loaf of bread to feed a couple of families, and he's on the run. He's been in hiding ever since. And he's not the only one.'

'You mean there are others around here?'

'Everywhere,' May leaned closer. 'You don't have to look far.'

I started to ask more, but she put her finger to her lips and shook her head. 'Not a word,' she said.

I took her advice. There was no point in creating trouble. But I still read reports about the Whiteboys in *The Illustrated London News*. They were classed as rebels, but I wondered if the people who sent these articles over to London had any idea of the injustice that drove these rebels to steal food. Why couldn't they all simply talk together and sort matters out in a peaceful way?

One afternoon, while Mrs Burgess and Miss Emma were out visiting, May and I were working in the sewing-room.

'Oh dear,' said May, as she rummaged through the mending bag. 'I've left the two linen napkins that Madam told me to repair in the dining-room.'

'I'll get them for you, May,' I said. Much as I liked it when May and I were in the sewing-room, I found needlework tedious and was glad to escape. 'I've never been in the dining-room,' I laughed. 'Where is it?'

Following May's directions, I skipped up the staff stairs and down the hall, nodding sympathetically to the sad, glassy-eyed creatures staring into eternity from the walls.

It was so quiet here. With Mr Burgess at the mill, the mother and daughter away and the servants downstairs, I could briefly shut away work and worries. I'd been here for nearly seven months now, and it seemed like an eternity. I hadn't seen Mama or Grandpa in that time, but John Joe kept me informed. They were settled into their cottage and they were well. I'd come to terms with the fact that Grandpa was working as a labourer. So I was feeling content with life when I turned the handle of the dining-room door. Now I could have a look around, touch things.

I stood at the door and breathed in the opulent fragrance. The long table was set with a fine linen cloth, ornate candlesticks placed down the centre. Vases of flowers on high stands softened the effect of the stiff furniture. What joy it must be to sit here and be served good meals in comfort! Did they ever wonder, as they spooned their game soup into their mouths, about the wretched people who would queue for their leavings the following morning?

It was only when I went over to fetch the napkins from the table that I stopped short with shock and disbelief. I shut my eyes in case I was mistaken.

But there was no mistake. It was there in an alcove: Mama's sideboard.

Chapter Nine

I fled from the room, my breath coming in gasps. I knew every twist and turn of the carvings, every brass fitting on the drawers and doors of that sideboard. How bad had things been, that Mama had had to sell the thing she treasured most?

With one hand over my mouth to fight back the sobs, I raced downstairs, through the kitchen. I was vaguely aware of Mrs Casey's concerned face and Rose and Betty stopping what they were doing to stare at me. I ran across the yard to find a place to hide. Some place that would swallow me up. Across the cobbles I raced, until I came to a line of stables.

I threw myself into the hay behind one of the stalls and let all the anger spill over into tears. I just wanted the hay to cover me. If I could just close my eyes and will myself back home…

I was startled out of my dark thoughts by a rustling. Peering around the stall, I was surprised to see John Joe. He had a white bundle in his hands and he was thrusting it into the hay, looking around furtively. When he saw me, he jumped.

'Esty?' he said with a note of relief. 'What are you

doing here?' Then he saw my red eyes and white face.
I wiped my eyes with my sleeve.

'What's wrong, Esty?' he asked, coming towards me.
'Has someone upset you? Tell me who and I'll…'

'Oh, John Joe,' I cried, running to him. He put his
arm around my shoulders and I told him about Mama's
sideboard. 'She'd never sell that.' I said.

'She had to,' he said.

'What do you mean?' I asked, backing away from
him.

'I knew your mother had sold it,' he went on. 'I had
to help load it on to the cart. Your mother told me to
say nothing. Mrs Burgess took a fancy to it when she
called on your mother. Now she's boasting that she has
a sideboard that came from the Earl of Kildare. At least,
that's what Mr Egan told Mrs Casey.'

'Well, that's it,' I said decisively. 'I must go home.'

'Shush,' he said. 'Try to stay calm, Esty. If you leave
this household you'll never get work anywhere. If you go
home, they will have an extra burden, someone else to
feed. You must stay. Don't you see? It's the only thing
to do.'

I pushed him away from me. 'I can't stay here.
Mama must be heartbroken over selling her sideboard.
I promised Papa I'd look after her…'

'It's a sideboard, Esty,' John Joe put in. 'It's a thing.
People are more important than things. Now, come back
to the house with me and try to behave as if nothing has
happened. Things will change – you'll see.'

'How will things change?' I said, wiping my face on

my apron. 'Nothing changes for the likes of us, John Joe. We're for ever at the mercy of landowners and gentry.'

John Joe turned me around to face him.

'Believe me, Esty, things will change.' He said it with such intensity that he almost frightened me.

We went back to the house together.

Mrs Casey looked at me curiously.

'Are you all right, *alannah*?' she said, wiping her hands in her apron and coming towards me. More than anything, I wanted to lose myself in her comforting arms, but I took a deep breath and shook my head.

'She's all right,' said John Joe. 'Isn't that right, Esty?'

I nodded, and went back to the sewing-room.

'Where are the napkins?' May asked. 'You've been gone ages. Why, Esty, you've been crying!' She got up and put her arms around me. 'Has someone said something?'

'No, May. It's not them.' And I told her about Mama's sideboard. Her attitude was much the same as John Joe's.

'If she did have to sell it, Esty,' she said, 'it means she got money for it, and money is life right now. Can't you understand that?'

I nodded miserably. 'But it was something so precious, May. It was her mother's. It was her claim to something better than just being his lordship's tenant.'

Curious eyes looked at me when I took my place at table at supper-time. Betty nudged Rose and grinned.

'Work getting too much for Missy?' she said.

I looked around for John Joe, but once more he was missing. He often missed lunch, but never supper. I presumed he would turn up late, as usual, and that Mrs Casey would have a spare dinner kept for him. But he never came. If anyone noticed, they never said.

The next day was my thirteenth birthday. I didn't tell anyone. There was no time for birthdays. Not like at home when Mama, Papa and Grandpa would celebrate. I didn't even tell May when we tucked our quilts around us and I read her bits of *The Illustrated London News*.

I was late for lunch next day. There was a strange silence in the kitchen. Nobody seemed to notice me as I slipped into my place beside Rose and Betty. Even they were tight-lipped. I looked around for John Joe, but he wasn't in his place.

Just then, the back door opened and several soldiers rushed in. One of them held up a white cloth. 'Where is he?' he shouted, shaking out the cloth. I gasped when I saw that it was a white shirt – the uniform of the Whiteboys. What had this to do with us? And then I remembered John Joe in the stable.

'Is it John Joe?' I whispered to Rose.

She nodded, without taking her eyes off the troops.

'Mr Egan knew they were searching the stables and sheds. He told us all to stay quiet about it,' she whispered.

We could hear them turning things over in the larder and the dairy. I swallowed hard. These armed men were searching for John Joe! Mr Egan tried to calm the soldiers.

'He's not here,' he said evenly. 'We haven't seen him for a while. He's not in this house. You must wait for the Master to come before you can search the rest of the house.'

One of the troops looked around at the rest of us. He shook the white shirt in the air.

'If any of you are caught harbouring a Whiteboy, you know the penalty.'

I gasped, as he ran his finger across his throat. Rose covered her face with her hands.

There was a frightened silence. When the troops had gone, Mr Egan nodded to Mrs Casey.

'You may serve luncheon now, Mrs Casey,' he said. 'As you'll gather,' he went on, 'John Joe seems to be missing. They've found a Whiteboy shirt in the stable. If any one of you knows anything, come and tell me.' And he looked intently at each of us.

What would he do? I wondered. Would he give John Joe up and be rewarded by the Crown? It was hard to know which side people were on.

'What about your brother, Rose?' I whispered, when everyone began talking again. 'Have they caught him?'

Rose shook her head. 'He was smuggled away,' she breathed in my ear. 'Far away.'

'And what about John Joe?'

Rose shrugged. 'Don't know. Don't say anything. John Joe's no fool.'

But that was no comfort.

Chapter Ten

Over the next few days the atmosphere was tense. Nobody mentioned John Joe's name for fear of inviting trouble. I'd lost my only contact with Mama and Grandpa. Now I kept my money in a drawer, waiting for the day when I could send it to them. I was caught in a no-man's-land of fear and speculation.

'I can't bear to think of John Joe out there, hiding somewhere,' I said to May one night. We were eating some left-over cake May had smuggled up from the ladies' afternoon tea. 'Did you know he was a Whiteboy, May?'

'Yes,' she said. 'Me and Mrs Casey knew what he was at. She always kept food for him. Her own nephew was jailed for stealing a sheep.'

'Oh!' I exclaimed.

May shrugged. 'At least he wasn't hanged,' she said simply. 'They were lenient because his father's sheep had all been taken to pay rent and the family had nothing.'

'What would they do if they caught John Joe?' I asked.

May sighed, and rested her head in her hands. 'Stop! I don't want to think of it,' she said in a low voice.

'I'm trying not to go to pieces, Esty.'

'What do you mean?' I asked, coming over to sit on the edge of her bed.

May leaned forward and looked at me. 'Nobody but Mrs Casey knows this,' she said. 'But John Joe and me, we're… well, we're sort of walking out together.'

'You mean he's your young man?' I exclaimed. 'Oh, May. Why didn't you tell me? You've never given a sign of it, either of you. All this time…'

'Because we'd both be sacked if word got out,' May put in. 'The Burgesses are very strict about their staff. Relationships are not allowed. It's a silly rule, but they pay our wages. We couldn't afford to be sacked. Where could we go, Esty? Unemployed in a desolate land. We'd simply starve.'

'So, where is he now? Where is John Joe?'

'It's hard to know,' she replied. 'There are many people who are sympathetic to the rebels. I'm sure he's safe. That's the only thing I keep hoping for. I just have to keep up a front and not give any hint of my involvement with John Joe. You'll have to help me, Esty.'

'Me? What can I do?'

'Just… be my friend.'

I put my hand over hers. 'Of course I will,' I said. 'You and John Joe are my two best friends. It's right that you should be together. I just hope he's far away.'

The days grew tedious. The troops came back a few times and it pleased us that they were wasting their time. We were trying to keep John Joe's name out of our conversations, but he was foremost in our minds.

Now and then someone would ask, 'Any news?' and we'd know what they meant. But there never was any news.

'No news is good,' May said. 'If he'd been caught, we'd have heard. So long as we hear nothing, then he's still on the loose, and the longer he's on the loose, the more certain it is that he's safe.'

Mr Burgess made an unprecedented visit to the servants' hall and preached about the evil rebels and how we must be on our guard.

'I have lost esteem among my peers,' he said, with a frown that seemed to go all the way to his wobbly jowls. 'The shame of having a rebel in my own household sits hard upon me and my family. I trust you will all do your duty if any information about this boy comes your way.'

'How sad,' May muttered, when he'd gone. 'I'm sure they'll choke on their sherry at losing face with their peers.'

'For shame, May,' said Miss Burke, disapproval tightening her face.

Mrs Casey's large bosom shook with laughter and she went off to see to supper.

I grew to hate the afternoons when May and I took tea to Mrs Burgess and Miss Emma. I found it hard to look at Mrs Burgess, knowing how triumphant she felt at having a sideboard that came from the Earl of Kildare. She would not mention to her dinner guests that she'd bought it, probably for a pittance, from the widow of a middleman. And I resented Miss Emma's total absorption in herself, her hair and her fashionable clothes. Though when I said this to Mrs Casey one day, she simply shook her head.

'The girl knows no other life, Esty,' she said. 'This is how she was brought up – how all young gentry girls are brought up. They know nothing else. We're all products of our upbringing, child. Just you remember that.'

For some reason her words made me very uneasy, in a way I couldn't explain even to myself.

'Calm down, Esty,' May said to me one night as I stood at the window. 'You've been like a chicken with no head for days now. What is wrong with you?'

I took a deep breath. 'I'll never settle here, May. I'll never be a lady's maid. You're lucky. You're able to do all the pandering and "Yes, Ma'am" nonsense and still keep your sense of humour. But as for me – I'm finding it hard to keep my sanity.'

May looked at me critically, her head on one side. 'What a lot of growing up you've done, Esty,' she said. 'In just less than a year, you've gone from an anxious little thing to a feisty madam with opinions.'

I laughed, but I had no answer to her remark. The anxious part of me was submerged in the business of surviving. When I lay in bed at night, all the worries about my family and the destitute people beyond the Burgess's gates fluttered about my mind like moths that I couldn't swat away – that, and my loathing of my mindless job pandering to the sort of young lady I'd once foolishly aspired to be.

'Just do the work, Esty,' said May, holding open the quilt for me to join her. 'Be like me. You get used to it after a while. You learn to bow and scrape without even thinking. It's simply a way of making a living. Some day I'm going to marry John Joe, when all these troubles are over. But until then I'll put my worries away. It's the only thing to do.'

One wet, stormy night, as we were sitting up on May's bed, an item in *The Illustrated London News* caught my attention.

'Look, May,' I said, pointing to an engraving. 'They've found gold in Australia! Imagine that – digging a hole in the ground and finding enough wealth to live in comfort.'

May looked up from the words she was writing in her copybook. 'How far is Australia?' she asked.

'Right on the other side of the world,' I laughed. 'A long way by ship. They say that the skies are cloudless out there and that all kinds of food grow. Listen to that wind and rain. Wouldn't it be wonderful to be where there's sunshine and plenty?' And no trouble, I wanted to add. But that would remind May of John Joe.

'Australia's not for us, Esty,' said May, suppressing a yawn. 'The good Lord chose to put us in a damp place awash with disease and starvation. I think he must have been tired when he created Ireland, and just took to his bed and forgot about us.'

'Just look at this drawing – this beautiful landscape.' I pointed to the illustration. 'All that, and gold in the ground!'

'You're a dreamer, Esty. Anyway, isn't Australia a prison? Isn't that where they're transporting some of our people? What can be good about a place that takes prisoners?'

'The prison is just one small area,' I said. 'Australia is huge. Just look at these pictures. The land is vast – hundreds of times the size of Ireland.'

'Go to sleep,' May said, as she leaned over to blow out the candle. 'We have work in a few hours.'

Lying there in the dark, I imagined being in that cloudless landscape. If only life could be like a storybook, where you had dark misery on one page, and then simply turned to the next page for scenes of happiness!

Chapter Eleven

Months went by, and there was still no word about John Joe. I could see that May was starting to give up hope. Once or twice I had to clench my fists when Mrs Burgess or Miss Emma complained. May gave up on her reading sessions, complaining of tiredness. And sometimes I could hear her snuffling softly in the dark. I tried to comfort her, but what can you say when things are that desperate?

One day, just after lunch, Mr Egan beckoned to me.

'Esther,' he said. 'Come to my parlour when you've finished your afternoon duties.'

My mouth opened and shut like a fish in a glass bowl. I didn't know what to say. The only time anyone was summoned to Mr Egan's parlour was to be sacked or severely reprimanded.

Betty sidled up to me as I began clearing the dishes. 'Looks like you'll be getting your walking papers, Missy,' she whispered. 'You're not up to service, are you? They've finally found out their mistake and are sending you packing.'

'I heard that, Betty Murphy,' Mrs Casey called out. 'You watch your mouth, girl. We can do without trouble here, so don't you be the one to stir it up, or you'll feel my slap across your cheeky face.'

Betty clamped her mouth shut, but not before giving me a satisfied smirk.

'It's probably nothing,' said Rose, when we both had our arms immersed in the sink. 'Maybe it's to do with your pay. Maybe they're going to give you proper money.'

Later, in my room, as I changed into my afternoon dress and fresh white apron, I wondered how I would get through my duties. Was I about to be sacked? Was there some bad news from home? The more I pondered, the more awful were my thoughts. I just wanted to run after Mr Egan and beg him to tell me whatever it was right now.

I wiped my clammy hands on my apron before knocking on the door of Mr Egan's parlour. All my earlier doubts came rushing back to my mind, especially the most likely one – that I'd be returned as a failure to Mama and Grandpa and become an extra burden for them. Perhaps this was heavenly retribution for not appreciating my good position here. Perhaps I was being punished for wanting a better life.

I took a deep breath and knocked.

'Come.'

No turning back now. Another deep breath.

Mr Egan was sitting at a small table near the window.

The room smelled of pipe tobacco, which reminded me of Grandpa. I hoped Mr Egan couldn't hear my heart thumping as I approached.

'Sit down, Esther,' Mr Egan said, indicating the chair on the other side of the table. He didn't sound angry. I sat stiffly on the chair, my hands clenched on my lap. Mr Egan cleared his throat and folded his arms.

'I've been observing you, Esther,' he said. 'You work very hard and you've adapted well to a life very different from what you were used to.'

'Thank you, Mr Egan,' I muttered.

He leaned closer across the table. 'I have some news for you, Esther... '

'What?' I was startled into interrupting him. 'Is it my mother? Grandfather...?'

'Let me finish, child.' He paused for a moment, as if wondering how to put the words he had to say to me. I held my breath. 'It's Lord Craythorn,' he went on. 'He's come back from England to his estate. He has decided to do a land clearance.'

'I don't understand, Mr Egan. What does that mean?'

He took a deep breath before continuing. 'It's something that many landlords are doing. They're clearing the small cotters from their holdings to make more grazing land.'

'Is he evicting people?'

'Not quite,' Mr Egan shook his head. 'He's offering them assisted passage to America. He gives them their papers and passage to enable them to settle into life in a new country that's offering good livings to those willing to work.'

I couldn't really see where this conversation was leading.

'He's offering your grandfather and your mother an assisted passage, Esther,' he went on.

I recoiled with shock. 'You mean, they're going to America? But they're not cotters, Mr Egan. My father was a middleman.' My words trailed away when I saw him shake his head again.

'*Was* a middleman, Esther. It's one of the harsh facts of life that when the breadwinner dies…' He shrugged his shoulders.

'They've had to rent a cotter's cottage – isn't that so, Mr Egan?' He nodded. 'But I have money,' I cried. 'I've been saving all my wages since John Joe went away. I can give them that.'

'It's no use, Esther. His lordship wants to clear his land. It's not a question of rent – your grandfather has been able to pay that from what he earns as a gardener. There is really no choice.'

'But they can't have agreed to go! They wouldn't go far away and leave me.'

'That's why I've called you here, Esther,' Mr Egan put out his hand to calm me. 'I have a letter from your mother which she gave to me when I visited yesterday. But I felt I should explain the position to you before you read it.' He placed the sealed letter in front of me.

I looked at it, afraid to read its contents.

'Go ahead, Esther,' Mr Egan said gently.

I swallowed hard and opened the seal.

My dearest Esty,

When you read this, Mr Egan will have already told you about Lord Craythorn's offer to assist us to go to America. After much discussion, your grandfather and I have decided it would be in our best interest to agree to his offer. Sadly, there is nothing to hold us here in our own country. With your dear Papa gone, we could never find employment and the money to enable us to survive much longer in these harsh times. I know this will come as a great shock to you, dearest, but we are looking forward to a future in a land where work is available, and where we won't have to depend upon the whims of a landlord.

Of course, my beloved daughter, we dearly wish that you could accompany us and share our new life. However, Mr Egan tells us that you are working well for the Burgess family and that you will be raised to a higher position in the future. This being so, we would quite understand your wish to remain in service.

Do consider carefully, Esther, and tell Mr Egan, who has been so kind to us and visits your Grandfather regularly. He will bring your reply to us.

Whatever you decide, my child, always remember how much we love you.

Yours, beloved,
Mama

I read through the letter again, scarcely believing what I read. Then I looked up at Mr Egan. I'd had no idea that he knew Grandpa, and was amazed to learn that he'd helped them. I wanted to ask him so much, but my mind was in such turmoil that the words jumbled together in my head. Mr Egan waited patiently, moving away only to fetch me a glass of water.

'You must think this through very carefully, Esther,' he said eventually.

'Oh, I've made the only decision I can possibly make, Mr Egan,' I said. 'I'm going with my family.'

Mr Egan sat back and smiled. 'I thought that would be your decision,' he said. 'But you had to reach it yourself. Your mother insisted on that. I'll arrange for your wages to be paid up to date. You may leave tomorrow, if you wish. The clearance is happening soon. You'll need time to help with the arrangements.'

'Thank you, Mr Egan,' I murmured, rising from the chair.

But Mr Egan indicated that I should sit down again. He cleared his throat and leaned forward as he clasped his hands.

'There's something else, Esther,' he said in a very low tone. I looked at him with trepidation. Was there worse to come? 'It's about John Joe.'

I covered my mouth to stop myself from crying out.

'I know I can trust you,' Mr Egan went on, almost whispering. 'Your grandfather told me what a bright girl you are and that it would be safe to tell you this. You know by now that John Joe is a Whiteboy.'

I stayed absolutely still, in case this was some sort of a trap, but Mr Egan continued. 'Before he found employment here, his own family was wiped out by the Hunger. He couldn't bear to see others in the same predicament, so he joined the rebels and began stealing livestock to feed hungry families. His crimes were not as terrible as those of the extremists who maim or destroy cattle in acts of hatred against their gentry owners. But unfortunately for John Joe, and others like him, they all come under the same criminal label. If he were caught, he'd face exactly the same sentence as the extremists, just for being a Whiteboy.'

'You mean, Mr Egan,' I put in, 'you mean John Joe hasn't been caught?'

'No. And that's thanks to your grandfather.'

'Grandpa?' I exclaimed. 'Is my grandpa a…'

'No,' Mr Egan said. 'He's not a rebel – though I imagine he would be if he were younger. I took John Joe to your grandfather the night I got word of the search. I knew I could depend on your grandfather – we had often talked of the sad state of the country when we met on market day, when he was buying supplies and I was overseeing the estate purchases.'

So that was why Grandpa would never take me with him on those market days! To think that he had a life outside the family!

'Your grandfather built a *scalpeen* near the cottage where he lives with your mother. A *scalpeen* is a hole in the ground, covered with earth and rushes…'

'I know what it is, Mr Egan,' I said.

'Yes, I suppose you do,' he replied. 'It is well disguised and John Joe is quite safe there – for now.'

'For now?' I put in.

Mr Egan nodded. 'Once they begin to clear the land, it won't be long before he's discovered. There is no place to hide in the open country, Esther.'

'Isn't there anywhere he can go?' I asked.

'America,' Mr Egan said. 'Your mother and grandfather have agreed that they will take him to America as part of the family.'

'What?'

'Once they have the passage fare and the papers from Lord Craythorn, it will be possible to slip past the authorities,' Mr Egan said. 'So, Esther, you'll have John Joe with you when you leave this land. Come to me tomorrow after your duties with Madam and Miss Emma. I will have your wages for you. But I'm sure I don't have to tell you the consequences for all of us, particularly your grandfather, if you disclose any of this conversation.'

'But what about Mrs Burgess?' I asked. 'Won't she wonder…?'

'Don't worry about that,' said Mr Egan, getting up from his chair. 'I'll explain that family matters have taken you away. Now, go and have supper. Act as normal, Esther. It is nobody else's business, what we have discussed here.'

Chapter Twelve

It was difficult to act normally as I sat in my place at table. Part of me was filled with excitement, and another part was terrified. But my most pleasing thought was that I was going to be with Mama and Grandpa again.

Betty and Rose looked at me with open curiosity.

'Well,' said Betty. 'Are you sacked, or what?'

'Shut up, Betty,' said Rose. 'None of your business.'

'It's all right, Rose,' I said with a laugh. 'Mr Egan simply wanted to tell me that I've been such an excellent servant, he's putting me in charge of the scullery maids. In future I'll be making the decisions about your duties.'

Rose smiled. Betty, to my eternal gratification, looked cowed.

Later, when we retired to our room, I could see that May was dying to hear about my visit to Mr Egan. I could scarcely contain my excitement as we settled under the quilt for our usual chat. May oohed and aahed as I told her everything – until I came to the part where I said that John Joe would be sailing with us. Even in the candlelight I could see that her face had turned white.

'He's going away?' she said. 'He's leaving the country? Oh, Esty…'

'Hush,' I said. 'I have a plan, May. Take that horrified look off your face and listen to me. My mother and grandfather are naming him as part of our family. I expect they'll say he's a nephew or something. The shipping people don't care, as long as they get their money. There's nothing to stop you coming too. You can be … you can be my sister. Will you come? Please say that you'll come.'

May stared at me, as if she couldn't believe what I was saying.

'It's a chance that will never come our way again, May,' I said. 'Just think, a new world full of opportunity for people like us! Please come. I *know* we can take you. If Grandpa says that we can slip John Joe in, then we can surely include you.'

May looked at her hands, as though seeking an answer there. Finally she looked up, a determined expression of her face.

'I'll do it, Esty,' she said quietly. 'I'll go with you. Apart from an aunt in Kerry, I have no family here. So, yes, I'm coming.'

We hugged one another with excitement, barely suppressing our delighted squeals.

'When?' she said then. 'When do we leave?'

'Well,' I began. 'Tomorrow night. We need to go to my family as soon as possible, to get things sorted before we leave.'

'Tomorrow night?' exclaimed May. 'I can't leave…'

'Shush,' I said. 'I'm leaving after tomorrow evening.'

'But what will I tell the mistress? She will be annoyed…'

'May!' I said, shaking her arm. 'We're about to change our lives! Will she lie down and die because you won't be around the next morning to dress her and brush her hair? I think not!'

May's eyes opened wide, then she smiled. 'You're right, Esty,' she said. 'Oh, my goodness! I can scarcely believe it. I'm going to America and I'm going to be with John Joe. I want to pack my bag right now. And my money,' she added, pushing me off her bed and thrusting her hand under the mattress. 'See?' holding up a linen bag. 'I've been saving for nearly two years.'

'You have money?' I said. 'Oh, May. That's good. In fact it's better than good.'

'What do you mean?' asked May.

'Don't you see?' I said. 'Lord Craythorn is offering us money for assisted passage to America. But if we add your money and mine to his money, we might be able to afford to go to Australia instead! Australia, May!'

'Australia,' murmured May in disbelief. 'We're going to Australia. America or Australia, it's all the same to me. I have no idea where they are, and I don't much care. I'm just happy to be getting away from here – and seeing John Joe again.'

It was hard to suppress our excitement as we went about our duties next day. Now and then we'd catch one another's glance, and smile. And once or twice I'd have a feeling of panic. Was I doing the right thing, taking May from the life she was used to and travelling across the world? But then, I'd console myself, the alternative was for her to stay here and languish as a lady's maid for the rest of her life.

After supper, I followed Mrs Casey into the larder where she was checking tomorrow's meals. As I closed the door, she looked around with surprise.

'Why, Esty,' she said. 'What's keeping you in the kitchen at this hour, *alannah*?'

'Mrs Casey,' I began. 'I've come to say goodbye.'

'What!' She dropped the plate she was holding. I bent down to help her pick up the pieces, and told her all. She sat back on the floor and looked at me in dismay.

'Australia?' she said. 'You're going to Australia?'

'I'm going to make Lord Craythorn listen to me,' I said. 'There's enough money to add to whatever he's putting up. He owes it to us – Mama, Grandpa and me – because my papa was such a good middleman. I'm going to insist on seeing him and putting our case to him.'

'But *Australia*,' went on Mrs Casey, getting up and wrapping the broken plate fragments in a cloth. 'It's so far away, Esty.'

'I know that, Mrs Casey. But I've been reading all about it. It's where the future is. I have a feeling about Australia.'

Mrs Casey was shaking her head. 'I can understand, *alannah*,' she said. 'You want to be with your mother and grandfather. But we'll all miss you so much.'

'Now don't go making me cry, Mrs Casey,' I said. 'I hate leaving you. You've been like a mother to me since I came here as a scared mouse with John Joe.'

At the mention of John Joe's name, Mrs Casey threw up her hands. 'That boy,' she said. 'I've been worrying day and night about him.'

'He's all right,' I said. 'He's safe.'

Mrs Casey looked at me questioningly. 'What are you saying, *alannah*?'

'Just … just trust me, Mrs Casey. John Joe is safe.' I couldn't tell her any more.

'All right,' said Mrs Casey. 'I won't ask questions. But … you be very careful, Esty. All right?'

I nodded. 'I'll be leaving tonight,' I said. 'May is coming too.'

'What!' Luckily she wasn't holding anything in her hands now. 'May too?' Then she gave me a knowing look, and nodded. She'd guessed. 'God speed to all of you,' she whispered.

'Best to go now,' I replied. 'There are things to do at home. The land clearance will be taking place soon, and our passage has to be arranged.'

'Oh, Esty,' she said, putting her great arms around me and smothering me in a hug. 'I'll miss you.'

'I'll write, Mrs Casey,' I said, trying to keep the emotion from my voice. 'I promise I will write and tell you how wonderful the new world is. Mr Egan will read my letters to you.'

She chuckled, and then set about packing food into a bag and pushing the parcel into my hands. 'Nobody will miss a few hardboiled eggs and slices of lamb. And here, what about some of my special biscuits? You won't find the likes of them in that Australia.'

I gave her one last hug and, biting my lips to fight back tears, headed through the kitchen towards the staff stairs. Rose and Betty were at the sink. I wished I could say something, but what would be the point? Tomorrow they would wonder for a while about our absence, and then get on with their jobs

I collected my wages from Mr Egan. He gave me a note for Grandpa and wished me good luck.

'Wait until the house is quiet, Esty,' he said. 'Then slip down the back stairs.'

At first, when I told him that May was coming, he'd been anxious.

'I'll never be able to explain that to the Master and Mistress,' he said. 'Maybe we'll just leave them guessing that she's gone to family somewhere. I'm sorry I can't arrange transport for you, but, with John Joe gone, I don't have a groom I can trust.'

'It's all right, Mr Egan,' I said. 'I think we can walk five miles. After all, that's nothing compared to the thousands of miles we're going to travel soon.'

He nodded and held the door open for me.

'Good luck, Esty,' he said.

May was waiting, her outdoor clothes on and her bag packed. We waited until the house was quiet. Then, with a last look around the room that had become our friendly refuge, we slipped down the back stairs.

PART TWO
Australia, 1852-1856

Chapter Thirteen

'You folks know what you're doing?' The shopkeeper looked at Grandpa with some concern as he totted up the bill. The shop was one of many in the harbour advertising supplies for the teeming crowds of gold-diggers who, like ourselves, had arrived from all over the world to search for a better life.

Grandpa just smiled as he marked off the list of items other speculators had told us to buy.

'One pick, seven shillings,' he murmured. 'Two shovels, six shillings each. Two pairs of moleskin trousers, eighteen shillings. Blankets?' He looked questioningly at the shopkeeper.

'Normally one pound each,' the shopkeeper said. Then he lowered his voice and leaned closer to Grandpa. 'But for you, old timer, nineteen shillings each.'

Grandpa nodded gratefully and began to count out the money. I put my hand over his and looked the shopkeeper straight in the eye.

'Seventeen,' I said. 'Make it seventeen shillings each, and you have a deal.'

The man looked at me with a frown.

'Go on, Mister,' I went on. 'You're making a fortune

out of the gold-diggers. Most of them are simply asking for enough for two, maybe three people. We're buying for a whole family. You can afford a better discount. We'll be knee-deep in muck while you'll still be here making money.' I smiled the smile I'd been using ever since my meeting with Lord Craythorn, and thanked God for my good teeth.

'You drive a hard bargain, Missy,' said the shopkeeper, reluctantly giving in.

For nearly two years I'd become well used to the business of bargaining. Most of our money had been spent in getting here, so we knew that we'd have to earn money to support ourselves, and save enough for whatever lay ahead of us in the goldfields.

Jobs had been easy to find. With his knowledge of reading and writing, Grandpa had got work in the Melbourne shipping office. John Joe had worked as a labourer, loading and unloading the many ships that came into the busy harbour. Mama, May and I had worked at the Harbour Hotel, serving meals and cleaning the bedrooms that teemed with passing prospectors – some returning to Melbourne now that they'd made their fortune. The tips we were given by successful gold-diggers cheered us up at the end of the long days.

Now, at long last, we had enough money to buy all we needed to go to a place called Ballarat. Grandpa had been told that the best gold diggings were to be found there.

'I was beginning to think we'd never get this far,' I said to Grandpa as we carried our goods to the horse and wagon that had already cost us a small fortune.

'If I'd known that, as well as tossing about for months and months in a stinking old ship, we'd have to work for so long, I'd have stayed in Ireland waiting on the Burgess ladies.'

'I doubt it, somehow, Esty Maher,' Grandpa laughed. 'We're our own masters now. Those days are far behind us.' Then he looked at me as I held the horse steady.

'What, Grandpa?' I said. 'Why do you look at me like that?'

He smiled and shook his head. 'You've suddenly become a feisty young woman, Esty.'

'Grandpa,' I replied. 'That little girl I used to be is a distant memory. If Mama hadn't sent me off to the Burgess's house, I'd still be a petulant young madam.'

'I know,' began Grandpa as he began to load up. 'But I will never forget your white face that morning when John Joe…'

'Hush, Grandpa,' I put in. 'I don't want to think of those days.'

'Well, sometimes I think of those days,' began Grandpa, before tapering off into silence.

So much had happened since the night that May and I had softly closed the back door of the Burgess house and traipsed the five miles home. John Joe and May had stayed hidden until we'd got our papers and assisted passage from Lord Craythorn. And then everything had become a blur of packing, and preparation for our journey to the far side of the world. It was exciting and terrifying at the same time.

One night, Mama had looked at John Joe with

a strange, thoughtful expression (he would leave the *scalpeen* late at night).

'What is it, Missus?' John Joe asked, looking uncomfortable.

'We're going to have to hide you, John Joe,' she said in a low voice. 'If someone recognised you on our way to the ship in Liverpool, we'd all be ruined.'

'I'll cover up my face,' said John Joe. 'Like I had aching teeth or … or a disease, or something.'

Mama shook her head. 'You'd still be male,' muttered Mama. 'It's males who draw the attention of the authorities.'

John Joe looked perplexed. 'There's not much I can do about that, Missus.'

'Yes there is,' laughed Mama. 'We'll make you a girl.'

'What!' John Joe exploded. 'Hold on there!'

'You know, she's right,' put in Grandpa. 'No one would bother an old man, a woman and three grand girls.'

May and I fell about, laughing at the prospect of John Joe in a dress and bonnet. The more we laughed, the more his stubborn face reddened. But we knew Mama was right.

The sun was just rising, the morning we left for Dublin to take the ship that would take us across the Irish Sea to Liverpool. There, we would board the bigger ship that would take us to Melbourne, Australia. None of us spoke as we passed along the familiar road for the last time. John Joe sat between May and me, wearing his bonnet and a grey dress of Mama's.

It was May who eventually broke the silence when she began to giggle.

'Why are you laughing, May?' asked John Joe.

He got annoyed when May pointed to his bonnet and dress. That helped to disperse the cloud that had been hovering over our departure.

'I hope you'll remember not to take huge strides when you walk, John Joe,' May said. 'You look like a true country bumpkin. And do stop scratching your head through your bonnet.'

'Don't heed her, John Joe,' said Mama. 'You look very…' she burst out laughing again before uttering the word 'pretty'.

Nobody stopped us on the road to Dublin – Grandpa had warned us to look straight ahead whenever we spotted troops.

We sold the horse and cart at the port, and boarded the ship to Liverpool. It was only then that we felt safe. However, Grandpa had insisted that John Joe keep on his disguise until we'd boarded the ship for Australia. There was only one tense moment, when Grandpa presented our papers and we were scrutinised for a few breath-held minutes. And then we were waved through.

'We're on our way,' whispered Mama, as we crossed the gang-plank, leaving European soil for ever.

Our tiny cabin during the voyage consisted of four berths, two upper and two lower. Mama, May and I shared the upper berths, Grandpa and John Joe shared the lower. We had a barrel for water and a commode that always stank of urine and, too often, vomit, no matter how hard we scrubbed it. That and the strong, sweaty smell at night was enough to make us nauseous – not to mention the constant up-and-down motion of the ship. The atmosphere was made worse by the clutter of our belongings. There was scarcely room to move. And often, we couldn't go up on deck for fresh air because of the squalls and storms. We were so glad to arrive, we'd have settled for any land anywhere in the world, just to be away from that ship after our hellish four-month journey!

And now, here we were at last, preparing for the biggest adventure of our lives. I'd never felt so full of life, so confident and grown-up, as I did shopping with Grandpa that morning.

'When we strike it rich, we'll come back and tell you,' I said to the shopkeeper, as he helped us to load everything on to the wagon.

'You folks be careful,' he said. 'The bush track to Ballarat is lined with thieves, bushrangers, convicts and sailors who've deserted. And when you do get there,' he panted, as he heaved the rolled-up tent on top of the pile, 'there's choking dust in the summer and filth in the wet season. And taxes,' he added. 'You'll be up against Her Majesty's licensing laws…'

'Look, Mister,' I interrupted, 'we've come from a starved land. We can cope with anything.' But his words stayed in my head as Grandpa clicked the horse into action.

We made our way to where Mama and May waited in the small wooden house we were renting. John Joe had made himself useful at the harbour by finding out all he could about the business of digging for gold. Sometimes his news was good, such as the times he met up with someone who had struck it rich and was on his way to cash in his find. Sometimes it was bad news, when he saw the defeated diggers who'd run out of money and could no longer pay their licence fee.

The licence fee was what worried Grandpa most.

'Why should we have to pay the Crown to dig holes in Australian soil?' he grumbled. 'Isn't it enough that they have driven us from our own land? What more do they want?'

'Hush, father,' Mama would say then. 'We're here. God will look after us.'

'No,' Mama,' I said. 'We're on our own. We've got to work this through by ourselves. Rosaries and long prayers won't pave a path to a decent living.'

Mama looked shocked. To be honest, I suppose I wanted to shock her. I'd listened to enough of her pleading prayers since Papa died, and I knew that, whatever was in store for us, we had to find the strength to deal with it together.

The night before we left for the goldfield, we stacked what was left of our Irish possessions on top of the wagon. Not that there was much. We'd sold all our furniture, Mama's china, lamps, pictures and ornaments before leaving Ireland, as well as our livestock – everything except our books. Grandpa had insisted we keep our books. Part of the money had gone towards our passage. The rest, along with our savings, was kept in a box attached to the underside of the wagon.

'That's all we have,' Mama said, as she patted the laden cart. 'Nothing but what lies in here.'

'We have ourselves, Mama,' I said, 'and we are everything we need.'

Later on, while May and Mama prepared supper, and John Joe was seeing to the two horses, I went across the open yard to where Grandpa was leaning on a fence. He was gazing thoughtfully up at the starlit sky. I put my arm through his.

'What are you thinking, Grandpa?' I asked.

Without shifting his gaze, Grandpa squeezed my hand. 'The Southern Cross,' he said, pointing to a pretty formation of stars. 'I'm told that the Southern Cross is only seen over the southern hemisphere.' Then he looked at me. 'We really are on the other side of the world now, Esty.'

His words filled me with a momentary panic. Had I done the right thing persuading my family and May and John Joe to come here?

As if he'd read my mind, Grandpa patted my hand. 'It's all right,' he said. 'I've been listening to the stories of over-packed ships taking starving land-clearance victims across the Atlantic to America. If they don't die of disease from those vermin-infested floating graveyards, they're lucky if the ships reach harbour. Look up there at those stars, lass, and make a wish.'

I looked up again at the Southern Cross and wished.

Chapter Fourteen

Grandpa and John Joe attached hoops from one side of the wagon to the other. Over these they nailed an extra length of canvas, which formed a cosy shelter for us and our possessions.

'There,' said John Joe, standing back to admire his work. 'A travelling palace.'

'Near enough,' laughed May, clapping her hands. 'But the real palace will come when we find all that gold.'

'A simple house with a garden would suffice for me,' put in Mama. 'We mustn't set our sights too high. Indeed, we might not even find…'

'We will, Mama. We're *going* to find gold. Please don't say we're not.'

I hopped up on the seat beside Grandpa while Mama and May climbed on to the back of the cart. John Joe rode alongside on his horse. We were on our way.

Once we were beyond the city boundary, the track became rough and bumpy, but that was to be expected. Grandpa was unusually silent, except for the odd click-click to the horse.

'You're quiet, Grandpa,' I said. 'You're not feeling

like Mama, are you? I couldn't bear it if you were.'

'No, Esty,' he replied. 'I know we're facing an unknown future, but we're made of stern stuff, us Mahers. We'll take whatever knocks we get, and bounce up again.'

'So, what are you thinking, then?'

He gave another click to the horse. 'Your mama,' he said eventually.

'What about her?' I asked.

He turned to look at me. 'Don't you love her?'

'Yes,' I answered hesitantly. 'Of course I do. She's my mother.'

Grandpa focused on the track again. 'Are you blaming her, Esty?'

'Blaming her for what?' His words were very unsettling.

'For your papa's death?'

'What are you talking about, Grandpa? Didn't I hear her trying to stop him from going out that … that awful morning? How could I possibly blame Mama for that?'

'So what are you blaming her for, then?'

I turned away, as if by doing so I'd stop him from seeing the lie I had just told. But I knew I could never keep anything from him. I took a deep breath.

'Going into service,' he said quietly. 'Is that it?'

I bit my lip and nodded. 'Perhaps,' I muttered.

'Ah,' was all he said.

We continued in silence.

'I was too young,' I said eventually, spilling out

the thoughts that I'd been trying to subdue since those long, suffocating days and nights in the cramped cabin of the ship. 'What mother sends a child out into service at twelve years of age? It hurt me, Grandpa. I'd already lost Papa, and then Mama sent me away to slave among strangers.'

'And look at you now,' said Grandpa, turning to me.

'What about me now?'

Grandpa smiled and switched his attention to the track again. 'You're all grown up,' he said. 'A headstrong young woman with some knowledge of life and the determination to use it. Where do you think those qualities come from?'

I shrugged. 'I don't know what you mean.'

'When you left, Esty – and believe me, it hurt me too – you were a timid child. You were spoilt...'

'Spoilt!' I spluttered.

'Spoilt, in that you wanted for nothing,' he put in. 'Sheltered from all that was going on. All the hunger and misery outside the estate – none of it touched you.'

'I saw enough,' I retorted, remembering Brigid and the day she fell down dead. 'I can't see where all this is leading, Grandpa.'

'Think, Esty. If you'd been kept at home, what sort of a person would you be now...? No,' he went on, as I started to protest. 'Think for a moment, before you answer. Think hard, Esty.'

I did think. If Mama hadn't done what she did, I would still be that sheltered child living in a grand house and concerned only with her own pleasures.

Just like Miss Emma. Going into service had made me realise that I must rely on myself to survive the knocks of life. I shuddered at what might have been.

'Are you cold, Esty?' Grandpa asked. I shook my head.

'Mama should have said,' I murmured eventually. 'If she had only told me that she'd asked Mrs Burgess to take me on. She did it behind my back, Grandpa.'

'And what would you have done about it, child?' he said. 'Tell me that.'

I shrugged my shoulders. 'Made a fuss, I suppose,' I replied.

'Exactly,' said Grandpa. 'And where would that have got us? Still in that hovel we had to move to, waiting for His Lordship to move us on to something worse while he fattened up his cattle? Consider your time in service as an education, lass. A tough education, I'll grant you, but an education nevertheless.'

'A moneymaking education,' I said, with a note of bitterness. 'Every penny I earned went back to Mama. Never once did she thank me for that.'

'Oh, Esty,' said Grandpa wearily. 'You have no idea how much she blessed your little head every time John Joe delivered your letters and money. She's a proud lady, your mother. Can you imagine how she must have felt, taking the earnings of her twelve-year-old daughter to survive? She could have done a lot better than my son… No, let me finish,' he said, as I tried to interrupt. 'I loved my son. I did my best for him, bringing him up alone when my wife died. But it was your mother who knocked the corners off him and made him what he was, a gentleman who thought about others. Don't ever forget that, Esty.'

I knew Grandpa was right. During that long sea journey, with too much time to think, I'd been looking for reasons to resent Mama.

'If all this goes wrong, Grandpa,' I said quietly, 'Mama will blame me and nothing will ever be the same again.'

'Ah, so that's what it is. It's your own doubts that are feeding you these bad thoughts, Esty,' he replied, turning to look at me. 'It's no harm to have doubts, lass. But to twist them around and imagine things like your Mama blaming you, and resenting her because of it, is a waste of time. Don't let that happen, Esty. There will be hard times ahead. We all need each other right now.'

For a few moments I thought about what he'd said. Then I sighed and turned to him. 'You're right, Grandpa,' I said.

He smiled, and lightly flicked the reins.

May poked her head through the canvas cover.

'Would anyone like a biscuit?' she asked, thrusting two round, oatmeal biscuits towards Grandpa and me. 'To keep you going until we stop for the night,' she added.

Chapter Fifteen

The first night passed comfortably enough. John Joe lit a fire near the shelter of some trees, and Mama made soup from bones left over from the roast we'd had as a sort of farewell celebration the day before. We looked again at the Southern Cross and talked about the future. The food and the warm fire spread good cheer among the five of us.

'Tell us again, Esty,' said May.

'Tell you what?' I asked, though I knew what she wanted to hear.

'About your meeting with Lord Craythorn.'

'Oh, May,' I sighed. 'How many times have I told that story?'

'Do tell us, Esty,' Mama urged.

John Joe threw another broken branch on the fire, making starry sparks light up our faces.

'When you crossed the bridge,' said May. 'Start where you crossed the bridge.'

'All right,' I laughed. 'So I stood at the bridge on the road to the Craythorn estate, and I knew that once I'd crossed it I'd have to keep going. It was terrifying. All the way along the avenue, I had to steel myself.

I just kept thinking of those pictures and articles about Australia in *The Illustrated London News*.'

'You knocked on the door,' May interrupted me. 'Get to the bit where you knocked at the door.'

I laughed again. 'I knocked at the door and a manservant answered. I said to him, "I wish to speak to Lord Craythorn." He looked me up and down and said, "His lordship is indisposed. If there's something you require, young woman, go around to the tradesman's entrance." But I was determined. I stood my ground and said – '

'I'm Miss Esther Maher, daughter of His Lordship's late middleman, and it is imperative that I speak with Lord Craythorn,' put in May, with a giggle. 'I love that bit.'

'Maybe you should tell the story, May,' I said. 'You know it better than I do.'

'No, no. Go on,' said May, flapping her hands.

'Well,' I continued. 'The manservant gave a superior sniff and tried to close the door. But I put my hand on one of the door panels – I was wearing one of Mama's lace gloves to make me look genteel – and insisted that I had an audience with his lordship.'

'Audience!' laughed John Joe. 'A regular lady, our Esty.'

'You learn a lot by waiting on the gentry,' I said glancing meaningfully at Grandpa. He smiled, and nodded. 'So I stared him out, the pompous old fool, until he sniffed again and told me to wait. It seemed like ages, but he came back and told me to –'

'Come this way,' put in May.

'May!' laughed John Joe. 'Will you let the girl get on with it!'

May looked at me, eyes twinkling, and put her hand over her mouth.

'So I followed him,' I went on. 'He opened a door at the end of the hall. "His Lordship will see you now," he said grandly. I said, "Thank you, my man."'

Grandpa slapped his thigh. '*Thank you, my man,*' he chuckled. 'What a cheeky little madam you were, Esty Maher.'

'Lord Craythorn was sitting at his desk,' I continued. 'He turned around when the manservant announced me and held out his hand. I didn't know whether I was supposed to shake it or kiss it. But I certainly wasn't going to kiss it, so I shook it. He smiled at me and asked me to sit down. My heart was pounding so loudly, I was sure he could hear. But I told him that I wanted to change our assisted passage from America to Australia, that my mother, grandfather, two unfortunate relatives and myself wished to make our way to the goldfields in Australia.'

'Unfortunate relatives!' sniggered John Joe. 'Hear that, May? We're unfortunate relatives.'

'Shush, John Joe,' said May, tapping his knee. 'Go on, Esty.'

'"Australia?" His Lordship exclaimed. "I've already paid for assisted passage for most of my tenants to go to America. Why should I make different arrangements for you, young woman?"'

'I thought of Papa and, somehow, I got a surge

of strength. "My father worked very hard for your estate, Your Lordship," I said. I was trying so hard to keep the shakiness out of my voice that my knuckles were white. "You know how he died. I know he would approve of my decision."

'I bit my lip, sure that I'd overstepped myself, and that he'd have that manservant remove me. He drummed his fingers on his desk for a few moments, and I held my breath.

'I wanted so much to tell him what I really thought of his greed and lack of humanity towards the tenants he was clearing from his land just to increase his wealth. I wanted to hit him and scream into his face about my father. But I clenched my fists tight and remained calm. There was too much depending on this interview.

'"You're very young," he said then. "You really don't know what you're talking about."

'"I beg to differ, sir," I said. "I have been reading about the awful, overcrowded conditions on those ships to America, as I'm sure Your Lordship has too. And I've been reading about Australia – about the fertile land there, and the goldfields."

'"You read, child?" says he.

'"Yes, Your Lordship. And I intend to live a worthwhile life in a good land. I owe that to my father."'

Mama was shaking her head. Even though she'd heard my account before, she still couldn't quite believe it.

'"You need extra money?" he asked me. I tried not to hope too much. He was, after all, a landlord who was only visiting his estate to oversee the land clearance.'

'Indeed,' murmured Grandpa, as he stirred up some more sparks from the fire.

'"We have some money," I told him. I was gritting my teeth to keep calm. "We have a reasonable sum for my mother, my grandfather, two relatives and myself. We're hoping you will provide the rest."'

'What a nerve you had, Esty,' said John Joe.

'Go on, Esty,' urged Mama.

'"You are a determined young lady," Lord Craythorn said. "And well informed, it would seem. Very well, out of respect for your late father I shall see to it that you get your money. Tell your grandfather to come and see my steward tomorrow morning at nine o'clock." Then he got up and held out his hand. I wanted to bite it and shake it at the same time. "I wish you a safe passage and good fortune."'

'Oh, Esty,' said May. 'You deserve a medal for your courage. Imagine, our Esty getting the better of a lord!'

'And here we all are,' put in John Joe, 'in Australia, on our way to dig for gold.'

Looking at John Joe and the muscles he'd developed during months of labouring on the docks, I marvelled that he'd once passed himself off as a woman.

'We really should get some sleep,' said Mama, getting up and brushing down her dress. 'We still have a long journey ahead of us.'

Before going into the tent I shared with her and May, I stood looking up at the Southern Cross.

I jumped when I felt a hand on my shoulder.

'Come inside, Esty,' said Mama. 'You'll catch cold if you stay out in the night air.'

Chapter Sixteen

There were times when the journey seemed as if it would go on for ever. The afternoons were worst, when the heat brought flies that buzzed relentlessly around our heads. Now and then, we'd pass broken cartwheels or discarded horseshoes.

'Where have they gone, these people?' May asked, as we stopped to inspect an abandoned wagon, its sides burst and wheels missing. 'Look, a child's shoe. They must have been a family. Where have they disappeared to?'

'Probably had to knock together a new wagon. That one was obviously overloaded and fell apart,' said Grandpa. 'What choice would they have? If you don't keep going in a place like this, well…' He shrugged his shoulders.

Mama gave a shudder. 'Let's move on,' she said.

That same evening, we met a couple of sheepmen and a stout woman who was sitting under a tree fanning herself with her straw hat. They'd stopped at a bend in the river to water their parched flock, which was guarded by a sheepdog.

'You folks heading for the goldfields?' one of the men

asked, wiping his sweaty brow with his sleeve.

'We are indeed,' replied Grandpa.

'Well, good luck to ye,' said the man. 'James Baker,' he added, holding out his hand to Grandpa. 'And my son Adam.' The son, in his early twenties, nodded. 'And my wife Rose,' James Baker waved his hand in the direction of the stout lady, who stood up stiffly and put her hands on her hips.

'Ooh, I shouldn't sit down,' she gasped. 'Too hard to get up again. Pleased to meet you all.' She smiled, and her chubby sunburned cheeks formed apple shapes. 'Nice to meet folks on this long journey.'

'You're going to Ballarat too?' asked May, looking with puzzlement at the flock of sheep.

'We have our gold right there,' said Adam, nodding towards the bedraggled flock.

'What do you mean?' asked John Joe, jumping from his horse to lead him to the water. 'Gold sheep?' And he laughed.

'In a way,' replied James Baker. 'Isn't that right, Tess?' he went on, patting the sheepdog which had come over to investigate the strangers. 'Wherever there are gangs of people toiling in the earth, there's hunger. And where there's hunger, there's a need for tucker. And, as master butchers from Geelong, me, my missus and my son will make our fortune with them there sheep. No digging in the ground for us, sir. We'll set up our corral and sell the best lamb chops at good prices.'

Grandpa chuckled, as he unhitched our horse

to drink from the river. 'That's very shrewd of you, Mr Baker,' he said.

We chatted some more. It was good to cool ourselves by splashing our feet and faces upriver from the sheep. We all shared out our food. Theirs was mostly salted mutton, hard to chew. When it was time to leave, they took a whole leg of salted lamb from the back of their wagon and gave it to us.

May nudged me. 'What on earth will we do with that chunk of boot leather?' she whispered. We both suppressed our giggles in our handkerchiefs when Mama responded by giving Mrs Baker a pot of chutney – sour and lumpy, because we weren't familiar with the vegetables we'd used to make it.

'Fair's fair,' May whispered into my ear. 'That'll kill them, and the lamb will kill us.' We smothered our giggles some more.

'We won't be very far behind ye,' James Baker called out, when we'd said our goodbyes. 'See you folks in Ballarat.'

'Those people could end up wealthier than many diggers,' said Grandpa as we moved on, leaving the baaing sounds behind us.

'Not us, Mr Maher,' said John Joe, setting his horse to a canter beside us. 'We're going to make a fortune. You'll see.'

That night we lit our fire on more open ground. James and his son had warned us about the dangers of bush fires and marvelled that we hadn't already set fire to Australia by setting up camp under trees.

We'd scarcely settled down for the night – Mama, May and I in the tent, Grandpa and John Joe under the cart, when we were awakened by loud shouting. Grandpa and John Joe were up and about by the time we'd wrapped our shawls around us.

'What is it? What's happening?' gasped Mama.

'Sshh,' said Grandpa, holding up his hand and directing his good ear towards the sound.

'Help!' a voice cried.

'Don't go,' said May, as John Joe made to move in the direction of the cry. 'It could be a trap.'

But when the cry rang out again, Grandpa unhooked the lantern from the side of the cart and edged towards the sound, followed by John Joe. Mama put her arm around the frightened May and motioned to me to join them. But I followed Grandpa and John Joe. I couldn't bear not knowing what danger might await them.

'It's Adam!' I heard John Joe cry out, as I caught up with them. Sure enough, when Grandpa held the lantern aloft, Adam limped towards us.

'Bushrangers,' he gasped. 'They came on us just as we'd settled for the night. Threatened us with cudgels and took our food supply. Made off with most of our sheep. Pa and me – we tried to stop them…'

'Where are your pa and your mother?' put in Grandpa, straining his eyes to look beyond the ring of lamplight.

'Pa's hurt bad,' said Adam. 'He stood up to them, tried to fight them off. We both did. And…' his voice tapered off as he looked down at his bloodied shirt.

'Your mother?' asked Mama, who had appeared with May. 'Is your mother all right, Adam?'

'She's tending Pa,' said Adam.

'Oh, this is too bad,' said Mama. 'How far back are they? We'll come and help.'

'No, Missus,' said Adam. 'Don't leave your wagon. Those thieving scum could strike you next.'

I shuddered at the thought. We'd been warned about these bushrangers – escaped convicts, mostly – but never thought we would fall victim to them.

Mama took Adam's arm and led him towards our camp.

Grandpa put his hand on John Joe's shoulder. 'You stay, lad,' he said. 'You stand guard at our camp. Arm yourself with anything you can lay hands on. Check that the moneybox under the wagon is well hidden. I'll ride back along the track and find Adam's folks.'

John Joe protested that he should be the one to head back, but Grandpa insisted he'd be more use at the camp.

'Let me come with you,' I said, as Grandpa saddled up the wagon horse. 'I could take John Joe's horse. Please, Grandpa. You'll need help.'

He hesitated for a moment. 'All right, Esty,' he said. 'But if there's any trouble, you must ride back.'

'Oh no,' put in Mama. 'No, Esty. Please stay.'

But I was already untethering John Joe's horse. 'Don't worry, Mama,' I said. 'We'll be back soon.'

We didn't speak as we raced back along the track. I hadn't ridden a horse since the days when Papa used to take me riding around the estate. And that was gentle riding, not this fast gallop. We had only gone a couple of miles when we spotted a faint lantern light ahead. Grandpa pulled up and held up his hand for me to do the same. We slowed the horses down to a walk and edged warily towards the light.

'All quiet,' whispered Grandpa. 'No reason for those thieves to hang around, once they'd got what they wanted. They're well gone.'

Still, we made no noise as we approached the light. When we were within earshot, Grandpa called out softly. 'Mrs Baker. Don't be frightened.'

'Who's that?' Mrs Baker's voice was tremulous. The flap of the canvas tent opened slightly.

'Maher,' replied Grandpa. 'We found Adam. He told us what happened. We've come to help, me and my granddaughter.'

'Oh, Mr Maher,' Mrs Baker sobbed, running from the tent. 'Can you believe it? They came upon us so suddenly…'

'Where's your husband, Ma'am?' put in Grandpa.

She held back the canvas flap to admit us into the small tent. I stifled a cry when I saw James Baker stretched out on a blanket. There was blood everywhere.

'I told him,' sobbed Mrs Baker. 'I told him not to go after those evil people. But would he listen? Oh no. Had to take them on, didn't you, old man?'

It was hard to know if she was angry or proud of her husband's bravery.

James smiled painfully at us. 'I'm all right,'

he mumbled through swollen lips. 'Gave as good as I got. Me and Adam both. And Tess too,' he added, stretching out to pat the dog lying beside him. 'She went for those beggars, didn't you, girl?' Tess wagged her tail feebly, worn out from the night's activity.

'But it didn't stop that lot taking all our food and flock,' said Mrs Baker bitterly.

'All your sheep?' asked Grandpa.

'We managed to hold on to a about a third,' said James. Grandpa turned to me.

'Esty,' he said. 'You help Mrs Baker load up. We'll move them to our camp. There's safety in numbers. Your mama will help Mrs Baker to patch up her husband. Right now, we must get away from here. I'll round up the rest of the flock.'

'Oh, bless you,' said Mrs Baker, putting her hand on Grandpa's arm. 'We'll never forget your kindness.'

When he'd established that James had no bones broken, that his injuries were mostly cuts and bruises, Grandpa took a lantern and the sheepdog and went to round up the sheep. I knew he'd manage that; I'd watched him do it so many times on the estate.

I helped get James into the wagon and made him comfortable. Then Mrs Baker and I threw everything into the back.

We could hear the bleating draw nearer as Grandpa herded the sheep in our direction. Mrs Baker hitched the horse to the wagon and we moved off.

I rode behind, keeping an eye on James. Now and then he'd emit a groan, but other than that, the journey passed off without incident. That's not to say I wasn't frightened; at every twist on the track I stopped breathing, for fear of attack. It wasn't until we saw the light of our own camp that I felt more at ease.

Mama, May and John Joe rushed to meet us, followed by a limping Adam. Even in the faint light I could see that he had been cleaned up and bandaged.

'After tonight,' said Grandpa, as he dismounted, 'we travel together. John Joe, help me to get these sheep together. We'll put up a makeshift enclosure until the morning…'

'No need,' put in James, as John Joe helped him down from the back of the cart. 'Tess will stop any of that lot from wandering off.'

'Good,' said Grandpa with relief. I could see that he was exhausted. 'Until we reach Ballarat,' he went on, 'we'll take turns keeping watch during the nights. We're in dangerous territory.'

Chapter Seventeen

The sheep slowed down our progress. We should have reached Ballarat after four days, and we'd now been travelling for six. Still, there was something comforting about having extra company. James Baker, in spite of his black eye, cut cheek and bruised skull, insisted he was well enough to look after the small flock. He and Adam, along with Tess, managed to keep them from wandering off the track. Mama and Mrs Baker proved their worth by making meals, while May kept the makeshift camp-stops in order. Me? I decided that women's work did not interest me. Papa had called me his 'strong sweetheart' and I intended to stand by that. I'd help with the physical work – herding the sheep, helping with the fires and making camp.

'Perhaps you'd help prepare a meal, Esty?' Mama said to me one evening. I was writing by the light of the fire.

'No, Mama,' I said. 'You three are doing very well.' I could almost see Papa nodding approvingly. 'I need to write something.'

'Write?' May said. 'Write what, may I ask?'

'A journal,' I replied. 'I've begun keeping a journal

of our travels. Not of the voyage. I was too sick and miserable to write in that cabin. This journey is what I'm recording. And I'll go on writing when we reach Ballarat. Some day, I'll put it all into a book and everyone will know our story.'

'Daft daydreams,' scoffed May. 'You're a lazy good-for-nothing, Esty Maher. Didn't you learn anything in service?'

'Of course I did, May,' I laughed. 'I learnt that reading and writing are the best weapons against the kicks and barbs in life. After all, wasn't it reading that brought us here?'

'Writing. Hmm,' May muttered later, giving the blanket she was spreading an extra shake. 'Just make sure you write nice things about the beautiful young lady who was your companion through all those travels.'

'Who would that be, May?' I said, and ducked when she threw a pillow at me.

Our banter ceased when we heard raised voices.

'Oh, no,' groaned Mama, 'Please don't let it be trouble.'

'I'll see what's happening,' I said, grabbing my shawl.

'No, Esty!' said Mama sharply. 'I forbid you to leave the tent. Whatever is going on, leave it to the men.'

'She's right, Esty,' put in May. 'What can you do if there's trouble?'

'I can *be* there,' I replied. 'Remember what Grandpa said about numbers?'

'Stop, Esty,' Mama went on. 'I don't want you

going out there. We don't know who…'

'Mama,' I said evenly, pulling on my boots. 'We're in rough country. It's not like home – sitting in a parlour and leaving the yard work to the men. We're all in this together. You can both lie here if you like. I'm going out there.'

As if to confirm my words, we heard Mrs Baker's voice among the male voices.

'Esty…' Mama began. But I'd already upped and gone.

Grandpa was holding up a lantern. Around him were gathered a group of men, some on horseback, some dismounted. I didn't call out. I just stood beside Grandpa.

'About five of them,' one of the men was saying. 'They're picking on small camps. They've already robbed four families of their equipment.'

'They must be the ones,' said Mrs Baker. 'They took our sheep and our food. Beat up my husband and son too. I hoped they'd be long gone.'

'They're keeping their sights on the track to Ballarat,' a rider said, patting his restless horse. 'We don't know where they hide out, but they know the territory well.'

'Thank you for warning us,' said Grandpa. 'We'll double our watch.'

'Have you any protection?' one of the men asked.

'What do you mean?' asked John Joe. 'There's me and Mr Maher and the Bakers…'

'I mean, are you armed?'

'No,' said Grandpa.

'I have a gun,' said Adam. 'Didn't get time to fetch it when they came – they took us by surprise.'

'Well make sure you have it ready now, son,' said the man who seemed to be the leader of the group. 'And move on as soon as you can.'

'Who are you?' asked Mr Baker.

'Peter Lalor is my name,' he replied.

'Irish?' asked Grandpa.

The man smiled. 'Indeed,' he replied. 'I came over two years ago.'

'You sound like an educated man,' went on Grandpa.

Peter Lalor laughed. 'Perhaps,' he said. 'But a degree from Trinity College, Dublin doesn't prepare anyone for this life, so we're all equal here, sir. These men and I are from the diggings. We heard from newcomers that the trail was dangerous and we've ridden out to warn people. Are there more of you behind?'

Grandpa shook his head. 'We're slower than most, on account of the sheep,' he said. 'If there were any within a day's journey behind us, they'd have caught up by now.'

'We'll ride back a couple of miles to check,' said Peter. 'We'll catch up with you folks later.'

We stood close together until the thundering sound of their horses' hooves faded into the darkness.

'Who were they?' asked May. Her curiosity had got the better of her and she came to stand beside me.

'Diggers,' replied John Joe. 'They came to warn us of danger. Those bloody bushrangers have robbed lots like ourselves.'

'Oh no,' groaned May, putting her hands to her face. 'I thought those thugs would be well behind us by now.'

'It seems they're everywhere,' grunted James. 'They know the land and can criss-cross as they please.' His tone changed to anger and he spat into the dust.

Grandpa was still staring in the direction of the riders. 'A Trinity man,' he muttered. 'Who'd have thought we'd meet an educated gentleman in the bushlands?'

May pulled her shawl tighter around her. 'Oh God,' she whispered. 'I'm so frightened.'

John Joe put his arm around her. 'Don't you worry, girl,' he said. 'I won't let anything bad happen. I'll break every bone in the body of any bushranger who comes close to us.'

'Come back inside, May,' said Mama, who had joined us. 'Let's try to get some sleep.' May let Mama draw her back to the tent. Mama looked at me as if she wanted to say something, but the moment passed and she followed May inside. It was Grandpa's turn to watch, so I went and sat with him under a gum tree.

'Will we be all right, Grandpa?' I asked, crushing a gum leaf and breathing in its comforting scent.

Grandpa sat forward and leaned his elbows on his knees. 'I hope so, Esty,' he murmured. That wasn't what I wanted to hear. I wanted Grandpa to comfort me, to tell me that everything was going to be all right, just as he had always done when I was younger. But I was older now and our worries were different – worldly ones, in a strange land. Soft words had no place here.

Chapter Eighteen

I must have fallen asleep under the tree, because it was almost dawn when Grandpa nudged me.

'Horses,' he whispered, getting to his feet. It took me a moment to wake up – my dreams had been dark and disjointed.

Grandpa clutched my arm and pulled me into the sheltering shadows. His grip became tighter as the hoofbeats drew nearer. We could see that the others had heard them too. John Joe and Adam had slipped out of the tent they shared and lay on the ground. Mama's face appeared, white and frightened, at the opening of our tent. She probably hadn't slept all night.

'Ho!' a voice called out. 'We're back.'

Grandpa's grip relaxed. 'Thank God,' he whispered.

The six men dismounted and approached Grandpa and me. 'Any sign of trouble?' Grandpa asked anxiously. Peter Lalor shook his head. In the dying light of the fire I could see his dusty, worn-out face. 'Nothing,' he replied, as he tethered his horse to the tree. 'They're a slippery lot, those bushrangers. They could be anywhere.'

His words made me shiver. Had we come this far,

only to battle with dangerous criminals who'd think nothing of killing us for our paltry possessions?

'We'll stay here with you for the rest of the night,' said Peter Lalor. 'In the morning we'll ride alongside for a while.'

'Oh, that would be good,' Grandpa said with a sigh. We settled back under the tree as the men unrolled blankets from their saddles and spread them out near the fire, keeping their rifles beside them. I envied the way they lay down and went straight to sleep.

'We'll be all right now, Esty,' said Grandpa. 'Why don't you go back and get some sleep, girl.'

'No, Grandpa,' I said. 'This is where I want to be.'

He shook his head. 'You're an impossible little madam,' he said.

'Good,' I laughed. 'An impossible little madam has a better chance of survival here.'

Next morning, everyone was in high spirits. The presence of Peter and his men made us feel safe and eased the tension that had made us all feel so edgy of late. Mrs Baker produced another salted leg of lamb and sliced it expertly with a butcher's knife. Mama fried some potatoes and onions, and we sliced and handed around one of our precious loaves. But we'd have given these men anything, we were so pleased to have them with us.

When we loaded up, they rode with us. Peter chatted with Grandpa as he cantered beside us. As for me, I rolled into the back of the cart and dozed. Lately, Mama had taken to sitting up with Mrs Baker in her wagon. May was walking with John Joe. It was reassuring to hear her giggling.

When I awoke, I was surprised at the silence. I crept to the front of the cart. John Joe had taken over the reins from Grandpa.

'He's sleeping in the Bakers' wagon,' he said, before I'd even asked. 'He's exhausted. An amazing man, your grandpa. I'd trust that man with my life.'

'You already have,' I said. 'Where are the men?' I leaned forward to look around.

'Gone,' replied John Joe.

'Gone?' I echoed. 'Gone where?'

John Joe shrugged. 'They went on ahead. We're too slow for them.'

'Oh, I wish they'd stayed with us, John Joe,' I sighed.

'It's all right, Esty,' John Joe said, putting his hand on mine to comfort me. 'We'll be all right now. Just two days to go. I'd say those thugs are well gone from anywhere near here.'

Two whole days. Two dark nights. I wished I could go back to sleep and not wake up until we arrived at Ballarat. I jumped down from the cart and walked along on my own. I tried to push my fears from my mind, but it was like trying to keep back a swarm of flies. I could hear Mama, Mrs Baker and May chatting, as their cart caught up with me. Mama leaned out when she saw me.

'Esty. Did you have a good sleep, dear?'

'Yes, Mama, I did,'

'Well, you needed that,' she went on, 'after riding off

with Grandpa and sitting up all night.'

I looked up sharply to see if she was annoyed, but she had resumed her chat. When I realised the resentment was all mine, I felt ashamed. I couldn't understand why my feelings towards Mama had changed. I'd hoped it was a passing phase, that things would go back to the way they had been before she'd sent me into service. But I'd never forget that awful day, and the thought of it filled me with guilt.

I looked around for someone to talk to, but James and Adam were behind with the sheep. I could feel all my emotional strength draining away, but I put it down to the loss of our strong escorts. I scanned the trail ahead in the hope that they might come back. They didn't.

Towards nightfall, we set up camp just beyond a grove of gum trees. The evening scent of eucalyptus lulled us into a certain bonhomie. Even my own gloomy spirits started to rise. The chat around the camp fire was full of hope for the future. It was well after sundown when we broke up to get some sleep. Adam and John Joe volunteered to keep first watch.

'Mrs Baker,' I began.

'Call me Rose, darlin',' she laughed. 'No formalities for me. Titles are not up to much when the living is rough.'

'Rose,' I smiled. 'If you like, you can share our tent. Then Grandpa could take Adam's bed.'

Grandpa stood up and brushed his trousers. 'No, no,' he exclaimed. 'I won't have that. We're perfectly comfortable under the wagon, John Joe and I. Don't be upsetting people with your bossy ways, Esty Maher.'

'Esty's right,' put in Mama. 'We ladies will be just grand together. You'll get a better night's sleep, Father. It's only for another couple of nights.'

Rose was nodding her head in agreement. 'That's a good idea,' she said. 'Besides, it'll be good to get away from James Baker's hog-loud snoring.'

Grandpa shook his head. 'Interfering women,' he muttered. But I could see that he was pleased. 'However,' he went on, looking at John Joe and Adam as they trampled out the fire to avoid advertising our whereabouts to bushrangers, 'James and I will relieve you before dawn.'

May and I moved our bedding closer to the side of the tent to accommodate Rose. Her extra bulk filled our small tent to bursting-point.

'I'm making things awkward for you, aren't I?' said Rose, as we moved our bedding around.

'Nothing of the sort,' replied Mama. 'After all, for more months than I care to remember we five shared a tiny cabin on board ship. This is luxury by comparison.'

May and I snuggled together that night, just as we used to do in that faraway time in our attic bedroom back in Ireland.

'If she snores too, I'll personally kill you, Esty Maher,' May murmured in my ear. 'Very slowly, with a knitting needle. And I'll salt your skinny legs like the Bakers' mutton and serve them up for dinner.'

'At least they'll be tasty,' I giggled. Still smiling, we both fell asleep.

I was awake before we heard the first shout – loud,

raucous and desperate. I felt a familiar tightening at the back of my head.

The shouts were louder now. We were all awake. I recognised Adam's voice.

'Dear God!' gasped Rose, clutching her blanket around her in the dim light. Mama put her arms around her. May grasped my arm as I jumped up.

'Esty!' she cried. 'Where are you going?'

'I'm going out there,' I replied, gritting my teeth to stop trembling. 'Get whatever you can to protect yourselves. We're not going to let those thugs get the better of us.' More than anything, I wanted to dive under the blanket. But reason gave me strength. I picked up the shovel we kept wrapped inside the tent and ran into the night.

Grandpa and James were running towards the tree where the boys were keeping watch. Adam was silhouetted against the sky as he rushed to meet them.

'They're coming!' he exclaimed. 'Listen.'

We stopped. Sure enough, from across the scrubby landscape we could hear the distant sound of horses.

'Maybe it's Peter Lalor and his men,' I said, trying to keep the hysteria out of my voice.

'No,' said Grandpa. 'He said they wouldn't be back, that we were near enough to the goldfields. Esty, get back inside. Adam, where's John Joe?'

'I don't know,' Adam cried. 'He's gone. He ran away when he heard the first hoofs. He's left us to fend for ourselves.'

There was no time to be shocked. Survival was

the only thing that mattered. Armed with another shovel, a poker and a butcher's mallet, the three women rushed to join us.

'Rose!' exclaimed James. 'Get back inside, woman. Can't you hear those horses?'

'I hear them, James Baker,' retorted Rose. 'And I'll fight off those thugs if it kills me. And, if it does, I'll take at least one of them with me.'

'Stand firm,' said Grandpa, as the silhouette of the horsemen became visible against the starlit sky.

May let out a muffled sob and clenched her shovel tighter. I wanted to say something comforting, but my throat was dried up and, anyway, what was there to say?

We waited.

And then we heard a loud shot that echoed over the dark plain.

Chapter Nineteen

The cry that followed was more of a scream. We watched as one of the riders tumbled from his saddle; the others stopped. We watched, frozen with fear.

Another shot rang out. More confusion. A third shot. Nobody fell this time, but there was shouting as they lifted the injured man back on to his horse.

'Peter,' breathed Grandpa. 'Peter and his men are back.'

The next shot made the horsemen scatter. We looked around for Peter Lalor and his men, but there was no sound other than the receding hoofbeats of the bushrangers.

Then May held up her hand. 'Hush,' she said. 'Listen.'

'Oh, no. Please don't let them come back,' I murmured. We froze again as we heard more hoofbeats. Just one set, one horse.

'It's all right,' a familiar voice called out from beyond the grove of gum trees.

'John Joe!' May dropped her shovel and ran towards the lone horseman who appeared.

'We thought…' began Mama, as John Joe

dismounted and patted his horse.

'Thought what, Mrs Maher?' he asked. 'Thought I'd run away?'

'Yes,' said May, honest as usual. 'But I knew you wouldn't desert us.'

John Joe laughed. 'Those boyos are just a bunch of cowards when it comes to the language of the gun,' he said, brandishing a rifle.

'That's my gun!' exclaimed Adam.

'Bet you didn't even miss it,' said John Joe. 'I heard those brutes while you were still asleep and decided to teach them a lesson before they reached us. I rode out to the next grove and waited.'

'You were asleep?' put in Rose, hands on hips as she glared at her embarrassed son.

'It's all right, Missus,' said John Joe. 'We took it in turns to nap. No harm done.'

'Enough excitement,' said Grandpa. 'What we need to do now is pack up and be on our way. They'll be back, gun or no gun.'

As we made our way back to our camp, I overheard Grandpa praise John Joe for his courage. 'Hmm,' he added. 'Where did you learn that marksmanship?'

John Joe looked at him. 'You don't need to know, Mr Maher,' he muttered. *Whiteboys*, I thought. But I said nothing. Never, during our long, cramped journey aboard the ship, had John Joe mentioned his involvement with the rebels. And none of us had ever asked. But, after witnessing his shooting, I wondered just what he had been up to.

'Let's get moving,' Grandpa said 'They'll be back for revenge, if nothing else.'

His words brought back that tight band of fear in my head. We scrambled into action. Adam, Grandpa, May and I urged the sheep along the trail in the semi-darkness. Mama and Rose took turns at the reins of our wagon and James led with his. John Joe rode back and forth, keeping a sharp eye on the trail. It was an exhausting ride, with each of us cocooned in our fears. The moonlight cast blue tree-shadows over the trail. The hypnotic lines of the gum trees kept sending me off to sleep – only to be jerked awake when I stumbled on rough ground. Now and then a possum would dart across our path. We came to recognise the undergrowth sounds of nocturnal creatures, but all the same, we didn't relax our watch.

At last the blue shadows were replaced by creeping daylight that spread along the plains. The first birdsong – a laughing kookaburra – eased the tension in my head. I was well acquainted with that funny noise by now. But then I heard a different, heavenly sound.

'What have you to smile about, Missy?' said May, as she caught up with me.

'Sshhh,' I said. 'Listen, May. Can you hear that? Isn't it the sweetest birdsong?'

May shook her head. 'Aren't you the daft one?' she laughed. 'Getting excited over a bird!'

'It's called a bell bird,' said Adam, catching up with us.

'Bell bird,' I said. 'That's just the right name for it.'

Now, other morning creature-sounds began to emerge, soothing away everyone's tension. But we halted short when John Joe, riding ahead, suddenly gestured for us to stop.

'Oh, no,' groaned May. 'Not more trouble.'

I squeezed her hand. We stood, our eyes focused on John Joe's efforts to hold his horse still. Then we heard a creaking sound and a wagon like our own eased into view. As it approached we could make out two people, a young man and a woman, sitting behind the horse. They seemed as startled to see us as we were to see them. John Joe rode towards them, but didn't get too close. I knew he suspected it might be a trap, and I squeezed May's hand even tighter. Grandpa left the sheep and walked over towards the wagon.

'Good day to you,' he said, his hands out to show he was no threat.

'Good day to you, sir,' the man replied. 'Are you folks going to Ballarat?'

'That we are,' replied Grandpa. 'And what about yourselves? Where are you heading?'

The man shrugged his shoulders and the woman was shaking her head.

'We're all done,' the man said sadly. 'We've been digging for months, me and my brothers, but we can't keep going.'

'Why is that?' asked Grandpa.

'The licensing fees,' the woman put in. 'We can't keep up with the licensing fees. We're broke.'

The man nodded his head in agreement. 'They are

demanding too much. My brothers are staying on to work for other diggings, but me and my wife can't stick it no more. We're heading for Melbourne to take whatever work we can get.'

'Oh, God,' I muttered. So they were right, those people who'd told us about the licence fees. Was this what was in store for us? Hard work for no reward?

They eased their wagon past us, and each of us nodded sympathetically.

'Watch out for bushrangers,' said John Joe.

The man looked at him and sighed. 'Can't rob us,' he replied. 'We have nothing they'd want.'

We watched them for a little while as the wagon creaked along the way we'd just come. Nobody said anything. No bell bird, however sweet its song, could eliminate the doubts that crept like icy fingers through my mind.

'So Peter was right,' muttered Grandpa, as he took the reins and clicked the horse into a walk.

'What do you mean, Grandpa?' I asked, jumping up beside him.

He sighed and turned towards me. His face looked worn under the leathery tan of the Australian sun. 'He said that many of the diggers are leaving because of the crippling licence fees. I suppose I knew that all along, from talk at the shipping office. But,' and he shook his head slowly, 'I just didn't want to believe it.'

'Grandpa! Is it that bad?' I exclaimed. 'What will we do?'

'Let's not dwell on ifs and buts,' he said, turning

his attention back to the road again. 'We can only do our best, Esty. If it all comes to nothing, we'll go back to Melbourne and find work.'

'Oh no,' I said. 'You know what that would mean, Grandpa. Going back into service for May and me, labouring for John Joe. Something menial for you. And as for Mama...' I shrugged my shoulders. What could Mama do?

'Stop galloping down Misery Hill, Esty.' Grandpa forced a laugh. 'We've come this far and we won't give up that easily.'

The sun was well up by now and the heat was suffocating. Grandpa pulled his wide-brimmed hat down over his eyebrows. I leaned back to try and get some shelter from the sun under the canvas. But nothing could ease that heat. I jumped down to walk behind in the shadow of the wagon. May had already discovered it. She was carrying a bunch of flowers.

'May,' I said. 'Where did you find those flowers?'

She held them to her nose and took a deep sniff. Her eyes danced as she looked at me over the tops of the red blooms.

'Adam,' she said. 'Adam gave them to me.'

'Adam?'

'Well, you didn't think it was John Joe, did you?' May said, with a sharp note in her voice.

There was no answer to that. May was right. We all loved John Joe as one of our own, but romantic gestures were not part of his nature. I hadn't really thought about it before, but now that I recalled the romantic stories

I'd read to her in our attic, I remembered the way her eyes would light up. *Romance.* I turned the word over in my mind and for the first time I realised what it meant. Then I laughed.

'What's so funny?' said May defensively.

'Romance,' I grinned. 'He's courting you, May. Now you have two beaux.'

'One beau, Esty,' said May, smelling the flowers again. 'One beau and a young man who doesn't seem to know I'm a woman with feelings.'

'Oh, May,' I said.

'Oh, May, indeed,' she retorted. 'You're too young to know about wanting someone who'd tell you that you look nice and look after you.'

'I never thought about it,' I admitted.

'It's all right,' May said. 'But if you breathe a word of this to John Joe, I'll dump you into the nearest river – and him along with you.'

Before I could reply, John Joe himself came galloping back along the track.

'We're here!' he yelled. 'It's Ballarat. Just over the hill. We've arrived!'

Chapter Twenty

May and I ran ahead as Grandpa and James urged the horses on. Adam was already way in front, his long legs striding up the incline. James turned to us as his wagon sped past.

'Hey, girls!' he bellowed good-humouredly. 'Race you.'

Rose waved her bonnet and Mama was laughing, as they leaned from the back of the wagon.

'Hop aboard, you two,' shouted Grandpa, making room on the front seat of our wagon.

'No thanks,' May called back. 'I want to be standing on my own two feet when I reach that goldfield.'

'Me too, Grandpa,' I laughed.

Holding hands, we stumbled after them. They stopped at the top of the hill. Mama and Rose climbed down from the wagon. John Joe had dismounted and was rubbing the horse's nose. Adam reached the top and stood with them.

'Come on, May,' I panted. 'They'll see it before us.'

Giggling, we joined them. But we fell silent when we looked over the place we'd travelled so far to reach.

Stretched out below us was a bustling township

of people, wagons, horses, even a coach and four that clattered along a busy street lined with a mix of weatherboard and fine stone buildings. I hadn't known what to expect Ballarat to look like, but such a civilised town was way beyond my imaginings.

A short distance away, in the area we came to know as Sovereign Hill, hundreds of tents were packed close together around high chutes on stilts, wheels and other strange structures. Smoke was rising from fires, voices carried across to us as we stood up on the hill. Mama had her hands to her face, and she was speechless. Rose's arms were folded across her big chest, an expression of disbelief on her face. Grandpa was nodding his head. Then a broad smile lit up his face.

'We've made it,' he said. 'Can you believe it? We've actually arrived in Ballarat.'

His words livened us up. Mama laughed as Rose hugged her and declared that we were all on our way to good fortune. John Joe whooped, mounted his horse and circled around our small gathering. Adam came to stand with May and me, but it wasn't on me his eyes were fixed.

'This is it, then,' he said to May.

I didn't know what he meant. May looked down at her bunch of flowers and said nothing. I wished I could say something, but my thoughts were all mixed up – joy at having got here safely, doubts about what lay ahead, and fear of the unknown.

I jumped, when Grandpa tapped me on the shoulder.

'What are you thinking, Esty, child?' he asked.

'I don't know, Grandpa. I'm feeling young and old at the same time. Isn't that strange?'

Grandpa chuckled. 'Not strange at all,' he said. 'You've had to grow up very quickly, lass. Too quickly. You're entitled to let your childhood come through now and then. I'm proud of you.'

I turned to look at him. 'Really?' The thought warmed me.

'The diggings,' James called out, pointing with his stick. 'Just an easy distance from the town.'

'And see, Mama?' I said. 'There are houses and some grand buildings. It's not the wilderness you thought it might be, is it?'

'We may not have one of those grand houses yet, Esty,' Mama replied. 'We may have to live quite rough for a while. Indeed, if things don't turn out well...' She paused and glanced at Grandpa.

I shook my head. Trust Mama to look on the bleak side.

'Of course things will turn out well, Mrs Maher,' put in John Joe. 'It won't be long before we'll have fine houses just like them. You'll see.'

'Why don't we go down?' said Grandpa. 'Let's see just what this Ballarat has to offer.'

In silence we went towards the busy town. The choking dust coming up from the street settled on our shoes and clothes. People stood to one side as our procession of two wagons and a flock of sheep stirred up even more dust.

'Shops, Esty,' May whispered to me. 'I didn't think there'd be shops.'

'What did you expect, May?' I asked, trying not to show that I was as surprised as she was.

'I don't know,' she replied, clutching her flowers and looking around at buildings that seemed to sell everything we could ever need. The delicious smell from the bakery reminded me that I hadn't tasted fresh bread for many days. May nudged me and nodded towards a dress shop; its fashions were just like those in *The Illustrated London News*, only these were in brighter colours, tastefully displayed in the window. There was an apothecary, a post office and a well-stocked grocery store. Mama was struck dumb again, and Rose was shaking her head at the wonder of it all.

'A hotel!' exclaimed May, nudging me again. 'There's even a hotel. Look, Esty.'

I laughed with delight. 'We'll dine there in our finery one day, you and I, May.'

Grandpa slowed down the horse and pointed to a neat building with a white front and decorative roof parapet.

'The Gold Office,' he read. He turned to us with a smile. 'That's the place that will help us make our fortunes,' he said. 'It's where miners take the gold to be weighed and exchanged for money.'

I could scarcely contain my excitement. I squeezed May's arm. I wanted to shout and dance right here in this busy street. We went on down the street towards the vast tented area, the goldfields.

At the boundary between the town and the diggings,

we put together a makeshift corral for the sheep, whilst Grandpa and James rode back to verify the documents for our digging site and for the Baker's patch of land for their sheep farm and butcher's stall. Mama, Rose, May and I settled under some trees. Tess, ever watchful, lay panting near the sheep.

'We'll have a look around, me and Adam,' said John Joe. They set off towards the diggings. We fanned ourselves and swatted the flies that bothered us.

Rose brushed the dust from her shoes.

'That itchin' dust gets everywhere,' she said, fluffing out her lacy collar. 'But wait until the wet season comes!' She rolled her eyes towards the sky.

'Why?' asked May.

'Why?' Rose echoed. 'Because, child, all this dust turns to muck. We'll be knee deep in the stuff, you'll see.'

But even those words couldn't dampen our glee. May looked at me and made a cross-eyed face that made me splutter with laughter. I knew that she, like me, wanted so much to go back and see that street again, to savour its smells and look into the shop windows. But instead, we had to mind the smelly sheep.

We were hot, sticky, fly-bitten and bored by the time Grandpa and James returned. Grandpa was waving a piece of paper.

'Here it is,' he said. 'Our plot. Eight feet by eight feet.'

Our plot. After all that travelling and hardship, we finally had, in that scrap of paper, our passport to wealth. The Bakers' plot for their sheep area and butcher's stall was beyond the camp, but near enough for us to keep in touch. That pleased Mama and Rose. I could see from her happy face that May was especially pleased.

Grandpa was strangely silent as we loaded up once more on the last leg of our journey. John Joe and Adam had been watching Grandpa and James return from the town. They made their way towards us.

'Eight by eight?' said John Joe. 'Is that all?'

Grandpa shrugged. 'Any more than that and we'd have to have another licence,' he said.

'So, no panning then,' muttered John Joe. 'Just digging, eh?'

'What do you mean?' I asked. 'I thought that was the whole idea. Isn't that why we brought shovels?

'We thought we might get by panning for gold,' Grandpa explained. 'The fee for diggings is high, Esty. We thought we'd make a start by panning, and then make enough money to buy a licence for a dig.'

'Panning means sieving the surface gravel in water that's washed down from the hills,' went on John Joe. 'It's called alluvial mining. But that's all been panned away. We have no choice but to dig ourselves a shallow mine.'

'Well, now we have the permit,' said Grandpa. 'All we have to do now is set up our tent and get ready.'

I sensed his apprehension. It wasn't because of the hard work – we were all used to that. It was wondering whether we'd find gold before the money for the monthly licence fee ran out.

Such thoughts weren't troubling May. Adam went over and took her hand to help her up. The light shone in her eyes again. John Joe didn't even seem to notice. I glanced at Mama and was surprised to see her smile at Adam's chivalrous gesture. But now there were other things to think of. We had to take our leave of the Bakers.

'This isn't goodbye,' said Rose, as she embraced Mama. 'When we have set up, we'll come and see you so often, you'll think we're family. There'll always be a discount for you folks, and the odd sheepskin to keep you warm.'

'Will you stop, woman,' laughed James as he rounded up the sheep. 'We haven't even started yet.'

Adam still had a hold on May's hand, even though she was now on her feet. They seemed oblivious to the rest of us.

'Adam,' called James. 'Let's get those sheep to their new home.'

Adam gave one last, lingering look at May and went to join his parents. Again I glanced at John Joe, but he was busy talking to Grandpa.

Chapter Twenty-One

We felt as if we were trapped in the Tower of Babel. The tented area was crowded with people of all nationalities. Some had built crude wooden huts with verandahs, which were raised above the dust level. The noise of many different languages mingled with the clanking of the machinery of the larger mining companies and distant hammering at the smaller diggings. It was exciting and terrifying at the same time. How would we ever fit in with all these strangers?

Nobody paid any heed as we guided our wagon between the holes in the ground to our plot. Children, most of them barefoot, ran wild between the tents. Some of them gathered curiously round us when we began to unload.

'Shouldn't you children be at school?' Mama asked.

'No, Missus,' one of the urchins replied. 'School's too full. Ain't no room for us.'

Mama shook her head and tut-tutted. The children simply laughed and ran away. Once more it was Mama, May and I who shared the tent while Grandpa and John Joe made up their beds in the now-empty covered wagon. Everything we owned was stored under the wagon and in the space left in the tent.

'Never mind,' said Grandpa, straightening up painfully after all the lifting and carrying. 'This is all temporary. As soon as we can, we'll build a wooden hut and have our comforts back again.'

Mama nodded, as she surveyed the limited space in the tent.

'A wooden hut would be a palace,' she said.

'I don't care,' twittered May, clapping her hands. 'We're here, and that's all that matters.'

'And you'll look after us men,' laughed John Joe.

The excitement on May's face froze for just a moment, but she quickly regained her good humour and set about unpacking some bread and tinned meat.

When it was dark, we sat under the stars of the Southern Cross and listened to the voices – some arguing, some laughing – coming from the hundreds of tents that surrounded us. Somewhere, someone struck up a tune on a fiddle; elsewhere there was singing; farther away, a flute was being badly played. Those sounds, and the hundreds of fires dotted about the goldfield, added a dreamlike quality to that first night. That's the way I like to remember our first taste of Sovereign Hill.

'I wonder what they're all doing now,' said May, poking the fire with a stick.

'Who, May?' asked Mama.

May looked up with a grin. 'Miss Emma and her ma. I wonder who brushes their hair and brings them their afternoon tea. And who mends their underthings?' she added, with a giggle.

'Why, May,' I said. 'Their hair will have gone so matted by now that birds will have made their nests in it. As for afternoon tea, well they've probably had to boil a kettle and pour tea for themselves, poor dears. Think of the hardship! And, regarding their underthings, they're so full of holes that the wind chills their nether regions.'

'Esty!' exclaimed Mama. 'That's rude.' But May's laughter was so infectious that we all laughed. A silly little joke, but it helped break up the overwhelming mixture of excitement and fear that seemed to infect all of us.

There wasn't much time to reflect on our fears after that night; it was straight to work for all of us the next day. Despite what John Joe had said, there was no distinction between men's and women's work. We all had to knuckle down. While Grandpa and John Joe dug the beginnings of our shaft with picks, Mama, May and I shovelled the rubble into buckets and carried them to a mound formed by other diggers. It was back-breaking work, made worse by the ruthless heat and the flies that continually buzzed into our eyes and hair. Sometimes we were too exhausted to undress at bedtime. We grew so used to the late night sounds of raucous singing and brawling that we slept through them – though now and then we'd jump at the sound of gunshots, as diggers fought over their territory or possessions.

'They're not all ruffians and ne'er-do-wells,' Grandpa said, trying to console Mama, who'd become visibly frightened. 'I'm told there are barons, lawyers, doctors, ships' captains, all sorts of fine people out there – even artists and poets, Kate. Good people like ourselves. We must ignore the brutal outbursts of the ignorant. All will be well.'

'Ha!' laughed John Joe. 'Barons? Lawyers? They're probably the ones causing the most trouble, Mr Maher. We know all about the brutality of the so-called "gentry."' He stopped when Grandpa nudged him in the ribs.

We soon found other things to add to our discomfort – spiders, scorpions, centipedes and relentless ants. We shook out our bedding every morning and hung it over a makeshift clothes-line to keep it off the ground. Even then, there always seemed to be one or other of the wretched creatures in the tent at bedtime. It was wearying.

I worried about Mama; I could see the strain on her face with every bucket she lifted. It was a relief when Grandpa suggested that she'd be of greater service if she'd leave the plot at noon to cook our meals and look after our camp. That meant more work for May and me, but at least we'd have a hot meal to look forward to each evening.

We blessed Grandpa's decision when we sniffed the aroma of her stew on our way back each evening. And the tempting smell caused banter among the other diggers.

'Lucky beggars,' the nearby workers would call out. 'Save us the left-overs.'

But there never were any. Mama, well used to keeping a good larder, bought vegetables and cheap bread rolls at the Ballarat grocery store and bakery, and created meals that made all our hard work worthwhile.

'Look at my hands,' May groaned one night, as she held them up in the firelight. 'I've seen sausages more attractive than this. And as for my face,' she went on, looking at me, 'if my nose and cheeks are as red and raw from the sun as yours are, Esty, I think I'll just bury myself in that mine shaft.'

'Well, you can start digging right now,' laughed John Joe. 'You look like one of Mrs Casey's boiled lobsters.'

'Really, John Joe,' said Mama. 'That's most ungentlemanly.'

John Joe laughed again. 'But I'm no gentleman, Mrs Maher,' he said.

'That's for sure,' muttered May, getting up and going into the tent.

'John Joe!' I snapped, getting up to follow her.

'What?' he asked. 'What have I said?'

'Oh, you're hopeless,' I said.

May was lying down with one arm over her face. She'd taken off her dusty shoes and stockings and her feet were calloused and red.

'May,' I said, throwing myself down beside her. 'Don't mind that silly idiot.'

'I don't,' she said. 'There's better than him out there.'

'Do you mean Adam?'

She raised her arm and looked at me. 'Maybe,' she said, 'and maybe not. Now leave me be. If I don't get my beauty sleep, I may be stuck with this face for the rest of my life.'

But, for all her toughness, I knew that May had a softer side, that John Joe had hurt her feelings.

Next morning, Mama surprised us by producing straw hats.

'I bought them from a nice Chinese gentleman I met,' she said. 'These will protect you from the sun. Tonight we'll sew some veiling around them to keep the flies away.'

'Oh, Mrs Maher,' said May, putting on the hat. 'That was so … thoughtful.'

'And you, Esty,' said Mama. 'You must wear yours too.'

'Don't worry about me, Mama,' I said. 'A red face doesn't worry me.'

Mama sighed, but said nothing.

But it seemed my head now had other things to deal with. That evening I collapsed with a fever.

Chapter Twenty-Two

For three hazy days I floated in and out of consciousness, my head aching until I thought it would burst. I was vaguely aware of cool hands and someone beside me fanning away the smothering heat and patting my lips and forehead with cool water. Someone who seemed to be there day and night. Someone who made me feel safe. I had a deliciously familiar feeling of being wrapped up, secure against the world. I was also vaguely aware of hushed conversations that came and went.

'The diggings,' I muttered one day, as I tried to get up.

'Shush, child.' It was Mama who eased me back on to my bed. She dampened a cloth and dabbed my brow.

'It was you, Mama, wasn't it?' I said.

'Shush,' she said again.

'You've been here all the time. I dreamt of cool hands – soothing hands.'

'My poor Esty,' she murmured, and she hugged me gently.

'Oh, Mama,' I sighed, and clung to her.

'I'm sorry,' I began.

She put a finger over my mouth.

'You have nothing to be sorry for, Esty,' she said.

'I do,' I said. 'I've been awful. I blamed you. I shouldn't have.'

'Oh, Esty,' she said, easing my head on to the pillow. 'You can't imagine how I felt that day when the pony and trap took you away. I had nightmares after seeing my little girl heading into a life of service. I've hated myself ever since. But it was the only way out. I truly felt that your grandpa and I would die, and I had to save you from that. They were bad times. So much death and…'

'Stop, Mama,' I said. 'Part of me knew it – that you were saving me. But the silly-child part of me…' I broke off.

'It's all over now,' said Mama. 'We're here in a new place and, with God's help, we'll find a new life. But you must lie in bed and get your strength back. You've had a fever. We think it was brought on by the sun and the bites of those strange flies.'

I closed my eyes. All that time I'd wasted resenting Mama for sending me away, and all Mama's time wasted feeling guilty about me!

Those few words had put us on a route towards more understanding. If only we'd talked about it sooner!

Mama smiled.

'I must prepare supper,' she said. 'No, you stay where you are, Esty,' she added, as I tried to get up. 'Time enough to go back to work when you're better.'

But I needed to be out in the open air, so I dressed and went to sit outside.

Grandpa, May and John Joe were so pleased

to see me up and about when they came home, that I said I'd go through it all over again just to see their glad faces.

'How have you managed without me?' I asked.

'Ever so much better,' said May. 'Nobody to get in our way and hold up the work. You stay there, Esty, and we'll have our diggings up and running in no time at all.'

'Thank you, May,' I laughed painfully through cracked lips. 'I'll do just that.'

'We managed all right,' said Grandpa. 'We hired a young lad, an Irish lad,' he added, with a smile of satisfaction. 'He was working with someone who gave up and left. Now he gets work helping out, going from dig to dig when someone needs an extra hand. Says he makes a decent living and doesn't have to worry about licence fees. So we've just finished the shaft and are almost ready to mine.'

'There's something else,' put in John Joe, his face beaming. 'Go on, Mr Maher. Tell them.'

May gave a little squeal and put her hand over her mouth, as she always did at times like this.

Grandpa put his hand in his waistcoat pocket and drew out an envelope.

'For goodness sake, Father,' said Mama. 'Tell us what's happened.'

May couldn't contain herself any longer. 'We found gold!'

'What?' Mama and I exclaimed together.

Grandpa held up his hand. 'Only a tiny amount,'

he said. 'Nothing to get too excited about. It was an accident really…'

'Hammering in a bolt,' laughed John Joe. 'Mr Maher was just putting it in when he sees this shiny stone.'

Grandpa was shaking his head and smiling. 'Not even a stone,' he said. 'More of a pebble. I took it to the Gold Office, and they weighed it and… ' he paused to open the envelope, 'it's enough to ease life just a little.'

Mama's hands flew up with delight and disbelief when she saw the notes.

'Well I never,' she said.

'So that's what you were all looking so excited about,' I said. 'And there I was thinking it was to do with me.'

Grandpa laughed, and patted my arm.

'Now we know there's gold in our dig, it'll be riches all round,' said John Joe. 'Riches! I've seen some of those diggers take bags of the stuff to the Gold Office.'

'Well, we have to find it first, John Joe,' said Grandpa. Then he went to the cart and pulled out the box where we kept all our money. He put in most of the new money and passed the rest to Mama.

'Two things to celebrate,' he said. 'First of all, having Esty back with us, and secondly, having found our first gold.'

'What's the money for?' asked Mama. 'We have a good stock of food…'

'A treat,' laughed Grandpa. 'Tomorrow is Sunday. I want you three ladies to go to the hotel on Main Street. Book a room, have baths, and put on some clean clothes.'

'Hotel!' exclaimed May. 'My goodness, I've never been in a hotel.'

'We can't afford it,' began Mama. 'Father, we need to save for the fee.'

'Yes we can afford it,' put in Grandpa. 'We need to reward ourselves for all the hard work.'

'And what about you and John Joe?' asked May. 'You've worked hard too.'

Grandpa smiled. 'We'll have a few drinks in the bar and join you ladies for a meal.'

'All this sounds so … so *extravagant*,' began Mama.

'Maybe,' said Grandpa. 'But labour kills a love for life, if it can't be rewarded in some way.'

'That's just fine by me,' laughed John Joe.

'Except that we'll be bathing in the river, John Joe,' said Grandpa. 'River water will suit us fine. Plenty of time to get dirty again next week.'

'I still think…' went on Mama, looking at the money in her hand as if it was some strange creature.

Grandpa put up his hand. 'We'll all be the better for this small treat,' he said.

May hugged me with excitement. 'Luxury, Esty,' she giggled. 'At last we can begin to live like grand ladies.'

'Well, it's just a taste, May,' I said.

'Oh, yes,' she agreed. 'But a taste will make us work harder for more of the same. I'm speaking of permanent ladyship.'

'Listen to madam,' laughed John Joe. 'It's far from ladyship you've come, May. The nearest you got was to tend to…'

'Oh, get along with you, John Joe,' Mama put in. 'A girl is entitled to dream.'

And so it was that next day we packed our bags with clean clothes and went to the hotel. The room Mama booked was small, but to us it was heaven.

May threw herself on the downy bed.

'Some day, we'll actually be able to spend the whole night in a room like this,' she said. 'Maybe lots of nights.'

Mama laughed. 'Let's take it one day at a time, May.'

We took it in turns to bathe in the hip bath in the small bathroom off the bedroom. Two serving girls brought clean water for each of us. We didn't know what to say to them, May and I. After all, we had come from a background of serving. I wanted to be friendly, to chat to them, but I knew that if I were in their position, I'd just want to get on with the job in hand and leave, just as I had always been happy to leave Miss Emma and her mother. Certain boundaries are hard to cross. And here we were, even if it was just for a day, tasting the other side of that boundary.

Mama broke the silence by thanking them and giving them some coins from her purse.

Oh, the luxury of stepping out of our dirty, dusty work clothes and into dresses that were clean, soft and fragrant because they'd been packed with the spare bars of soap from the trader in the harbour! 'I feel like a princess,' laughed May. 'At least, on the inside,' she added, looking into the mirror. 'Whatever can we do about our sunburnt faces and rough hands?'

'We *are* princesses, May,' agreed Mama. 'For now. So let's join our princes downstairs.'

It didn't matter that there were much grander ladies in the dining-room with dresses straight out of Miss Emma's fashion pages. And it didn't matter that our princes wore creased shirts and jackets that hadn't quite had all the dust thumped out of them. This was our first treat since we'd left Ireland, and we were excited. We'd found gold!

Grandpa stood up as we approached, and tapped John Joe on the shoulder to do likewise.

We were served chicken soup, mutton with carrots and an orange-coloured vegetable.

'What is this?' asked John Joe, poking at the vegetable.

Grandpa looked at the menu. 'Pumpkin,' he read out.

'Never heard of it,' said John Joe, sniffing it suspiciously.

'Best get used to it, lad,' laughed Grandpa. 'Best get used to lots of things we didn't have back home.'

There was a slight awkwardness at the mention of home, as we remembered the Hunger, and the destitutes who would have been grateful for even a mouthful of pumpkin soup. The moment was relieved by the sudden appearance of James Baker and Adam. After a warm welcome, they pulled up chairs and sat with us. I smiled, as Adam pulled his chair close to May's. She looked at me and blushed.

Grandpa told them of our find and they were as excited as we were, which made us happy all over again. Adam told us that they had almost finished building their 'butcher's shambles'.

'Shambles?' asked Mama.

James laughed. 'That's what they call a butcher's stall,' he explained. 'It's just a crude hut, really. It has to be a distance from the town…'

'On account of the smell,' put in Adam. 'But my pa is such a good butcher,' he went on proudly, 'that there will be no smells from Baker and Son, Superior Butchers, when we're rich enough to open a proper shop right in the middle of Ballarat.'

'Indeed. It's a start,' added James. 'Like you and your gold pebble, we'll move on to greater things.'

'Where is your mother, Adam?' asked Mama. 'Is she well?'

'She's very well, thank you, Ma'am,' replied Adam. 'In fact, she will be meeting us here shortly.'

Suddenly, all the chatter in the dining-room stopped and some soldiers in red uniforms entered.

'Queen's troops,' muttered James.

Grandpa turned to look at the soldiers. I must say, I thought they were splendid in their bright uniforms. If they noticed the hushed response to their presence, it didn't seem to bother them. Gradually conversation returned, a little more subdued, and we forgot about the momentary *frisson* of disapproval, especially when we were served sponge pudding with marmalade sauce. Mama was cheered when Mrs Baker sailed in with bags of shopping and a cheery smile.

'This is the best day ever,' May whispered to me.

The troops fascinated me. I had never seen anyone in uniform up close before. Were these the people who were so hated in my old country? Surely such handsome men couldn't be so terrible? I blinked, when I saw that a young trooper who couldn't have been more than seventeen years old was staring back. I blushed, just like May, and switched my attention to the people at my own table. Mama and Rose were discussing the camp, May and Adam were chatting, Grandpa, James and John Joe were deep in conversation.

I looked again. The young man was still staring at me. He couldn't be looking at me, I thought. Why would anyone want to look at me with my scorched face and wild hair? Yet I was disappointed when the troops eventually left the dining-room.

'People come in here,' explained James, 'because it can get rowdy in the bar. There's them who can't bear to be in the same room as those troops.'

The soldiers had scarcely been gone ten minutes when another group of men entered.

'It's Peter!' exclaimed Grandpa. 'Peter Lalor.'

He was accompanied by several other serious-looking men. They chose a table at the far end of the dining-room.

'That's Henry Seekamp with him,' whispered James. 'He runs *The Ballarat Times*. I'm told he gets into trouble with the authorities for siding with the diggers in his paper. They say he'll be closed down if he doesn't pull in his horns.'

'What does he write about?' asked Grandpa.

James leaned closer to Grandpa. 'Justice for the diggers,' he murmured.

Grandpa looked at James with admiration. 'You know a lot, considering you've been here only as long as we have,' he said.

James tapped his nose conspiratorially. 'I'm a businessman,' he said. 'It's my business to know who's who in an up-and-coming town. I listen and I learn.'

'And what else have you learned?' laughed Grandpa.

'There's trouble coming,' replied James. 'Big trouble.'

Chapter Twenty-Three

We tasted some of that trouble a couple of days later.

Grandpa and John Joe had finished the shaft and were now mining, aided by Mike, the Irish lad. Mike didn't talk much.

'Best not to ask questions,' Grandpa said, when my curiosity got the better of me. 'He may have something to hide.'

'What could he have to hide?' I wondered aloud.

'Transportation,' John Joe said. 'He could be a convict who got away. But even I wouldn't ask him.'

So Mike did his work quietly and took his share of our packed lunch to a spot some distance from the rest of us. The work we did was slow and laborious. Using a windlass – a sort of hoist – Grandpa raised a bucket filled with the gravel chippings he hammered from the shaft. Mike shovelled them into buckets which Mama, May and I emptied into a wooden barrow. Then May and I took the barrow of gravel to the creek where John Joe washed it to separate any gold. Each day Mama would leave at noon, and it pleased me when I'd see the strained look leave her face. Still, we felt her absence as the work increased. We were like automatons, each act dictated by habit rather than thought. The only noise we were conscious of was the bullock horn that was blown by the mining companies, to announce a change of shifts. But there was no change of shift for us. It was all hard graft.

One day, as May and I returned from the creek, we were surprised to see two troopers on horseback at our shaft. One of them was shouting down the entrance. As we drew closer, Grandpa's head appeared.

'About time, you old goat,' the trooper shouted at him. 'Licence. Now!'

I'd never seen Grandpa looking so anxious, and it frightened me. 'Here,' he said.

With a swoop, the trooper whipped the papers from Grandpa's hand. The younger trooper wrote something into a notebook. He turned as May and I approached, and I was taken aback to see that it was the young man who'd stared at me in the hotel. My heart sank. Was this all he amounted to in his grand uniform – demanding money from hard workers like my grandfather?

The exchange was over in moments, but as the young trooper followed his rough companion, he turned and gave me a sympathetic look.

'Scum,' grunted Grandpa. 'All they had to do was ask. There was no need to insult us as if we were thieves and ne'er-do-wells.'

The young trooper gave me one last look before riding away.

For reasons I found hard to explain to May, I could not respond to her cheerful chatter for the rest of the day. Something seemed to have died inside me. Silly, I thought, emptying my bucket. Silly me, for thinking that a young officer in a red uniform would want to stare at me. And sillier still to be resentful about someone who was involved in such unjust duties.

Later that night, as we sat at our fire, Grandpa still looked upset.

'It's not the bloomin' licence fee,' he said. 'Even though I know that every digger is up in arms about paying such high fees to the English Crown. It's something we have to do, so we do it because the whole colony belongs to them. It's the way they shout at us. I've heard them bellow insults down other shafts and it's distressing. Almost as bad as hitting us.'

There was nothing any of us could say. We finished our meal in silence and went to bed. That night was particularly rowdy – something we'd have to get accustomed to after licence inspection days.

May reached across and took my hand.

'Don't worry, Esty,' she said. 'This will all end in better things.'

I wished I could believe her. But I knew that, now we'd had a taste of verbal aggression, Grandpa's anxiety about the licence money would continue to haunt him. John Joe took to leaving us after work, and not returning until very late. May asked him once where he disappeared to, but he just shook his head and replied, 'Men's affairs, May.'

'Hm,' May snorted. 'I can imagine what sort of affairs they'd be.'

'Nothing for you to worry about,' John Joe laughed.

'As if I would,' May retorted. But I could see that she was annoyed.

Later that night, when I knew Mama was asleep, I nudged May. 'What's upsetting you?' I asked her. 'Is it John Joe? I thought you were interested in Adam.'

'I am, and I'm not,' she whispered. 'I don't know what to think.'

'Are you still carrying a torch for John Joe?'

May gave an exasperated sigh and raised herself to look at me in the candlelight.

'It's complicated, Esty,' she said. 'When we were in service, John Joe and me, well, we were sort of thrown together. He was really the only one I felt comfortable with in that world. We hit it off when we first met – I was a kitchen maid at thirteen, and he was a stable lad. I used to smuggle treats to him. There was no romance. We just muddled along. It was sort of accepted between us that we'd eventually end up together when the time was right. Do you know' – she paused and looked bashful – 'we've never even kissed.'

'Get away with you!' I exclaimed, then looked over to see if I'd woken Mama. 'I can't believe that.'

'It's true,' went on May. 'We had to keep up the secrecy in case we were sacked. We only got to talk now and then, in the stables or in the pantry. It's only now I realise that John Joe's priorities are different from mine. He's always been up to something – like the Whiteboys – and he'd never tell me anything. I didn't know any better then. But I do now.'

'Because of Adam?'

She nodded. 'Esty, can you imagine what it's like to be treated as someone special? To be given flowers and be told how nice you look – even if you know you look like a dried plum? I've never even dreamt that being a woman can mean that sort of thing. And I like it very much. I want more of it. I really do.'

That was a long speech for May. I could see the sparkle in her eyes. 'So what's the problem?' I asked.

May sighed and picked at the threads on her blanket. 'I don't want to hurt John Joe,' she whispered. 'I know he treats me like a piece of old furniture, but I keep remembering how we were always there for one another all the time we were in service. He made my life easier. And I thought that was what love was all about. But now…' she sighed. 'Now I know that there's more to love. Do I sound like a fool?'

'Not at all,' I replied, giving her a reassuring squeeze. 'Adam is smitten. I could see that when we were travelling together. He's a really nice fellow, May. And he makes no secret of the fact that he admires you. There's no point in trying to hide your feelings for him from John Joe. Anyway, to be fair, you'll be leaving John Joe free to find someone else. You can't keep playing both of them along, or you'll end up with neither.'

'I suppose you're right,' she murmured.

'Quite right,' came Mama's voice from the other side of the tent.

Chapter Twenty-Four

Now that I was back at work, Grandpa insisted that Mama should stay away from the diggings altogether.

'We're managing very well, Kate. Especially now that Esty is strong again,' he said, as we were sitting at our campfire. John Joe had disappeared again after supper, but we'd come to expect that now. 'It's not work for a mother…'

'Are you suggesting I can't carry a bucket of earth from one place to another?' said Mama. 'Really, Father!'

It was so unusual to see Grandpa stuck for words that I tried not to giggle.

'Well, no, no, Kate,' he stuttered. 'Not at all. It's just not right for a lady. All that mucking about…'

'But you think it's all right for me and Esty,' put in May. 'Hm.'

'Well, you're young,' went on Grandpa. 'I mean, you girls are strong…'

'Oh, Grandpa,' I laughed. 'Get to the point.'

But Mama was standing her ground.

'You mean, you want me to stay here and do nothing?' she said. 'What's wrong with me working my shift at the diggings and leaving early to cook?

'No,' Grandpa insisted. 'Cook, yes. But,' he paused, and shuffled a bit, 'Patrick wouldn't like the other work,' he muttered. 'Not now, when we have help.'

Well, his mention of Papa silenced all of us. I looked at Mama and tried to remember her as she was before all our troubles, with her hair neat, her clothes clean and elegant, her hands white and her face serene. Now the sun had etched deep lines in her face, her hair had faded to a brownish-grey, and her shoulders were stooped from work and anxiety. For the first time I realised she was worn out. I was shocked, and I also felt guilty. Papa's last words to me had been to look after Mama. I wanted to reach out and hug her. But I couldn't – I would have felt awkward. Mama had never been the hugging sort – except when I was ill.

'He's right, Mama,' I said. 'We're managing well enough. We have a routine and the work is not so bad.'

May picked up on my words. 'That's true, Mrs Maher,' she said. 'We're doing well, me, Esty and Mike. We keep John Joe supplied with gravel at the creek while Mr Maher hammers away down the shaft.'

Mama sniffed. 'Well, if that's how you all feel,' she said, getting up from the log seat John Joe had made for her. 'I'll just take my old bones to bed.'

I looked at Grandpa's face. It was stamped with uncertainty and embarrassment.

'You're right, Grandpa,' I said. 'Mama is exhausted. She'll come round to our way of thinking.'

'Do you think so?' he asked. 'She wasn't cut out for this, Esty. She's had enough hardship during the past couple of years. But,' he added, looking at me with a grin, 'you're a fiery madam who can take all life's knocks and bounce back. I know that, for sure.'

'And that's the truth,' said May. 'It's thanks to you we're not all lying dead in a hole in the ground back home.'

Now I was embarrassed by their words. 'Instead, we're half-dead from shifting muck from a hole in the ground,' I joked.

It was much later that night that I heard hushed voices outside. I peeped under the canvas and saw Grandpa and John Joe silhouetted against the dying campfire. I strained to hear what they were saying, but could only make out disjointed words – Peter Lalor … protest … licence fees … corruption … I was too tired to make any sense of it. Besides, we had found our first gold and good things were happening.

'All's right with the world, Papa,' I whispered to the Southern Cross, partly visible through the top flap we left open at nights to let in the cool air.

But my optimism was soon to be shattered.

Chapter Twenty-Five

Some days later, Mike cut his hand on a piece of jagged stone. He tried to staunch the flow of blood by tucking his hand under his arm.

'Go up to our tent, lad,' urged Grandpa. 'Ask Mrs Maher to clean and bind that wound. Go on, now,' he added, when Mike began to protest. 'Can't have you bleeding to death in our digging.'

Mike did as he was told. We were surprised when he didn't come back before we finished for the evening.

'Must have been a bad gash,' said Grandpa, as we made our way through the camp. 'Knowing your Mama, she's probably feeding him some of that delicious dinner I'm smelling.'

But when we reached our tent, there was no sign of Mike.

'Where have you hidden the boy?' asked Grandpa.

'What do you mean?' Mama looked puzzled as she set out dishes on the wooden table Grandpa had made. 'What boy?'

'Mike,' said John Joe, washing his hands in the basin outside the tent.

'Mike?' said Mama. 'What about him?'

'We sent him to you,' replied Grandpa. 'He cut his hand and I sent him to you to clean the cut and bandage it. A lad like that wouldn't know how to deal with an injury.'

Mama ladled out the stew. 'He didn't come,' she said. 'But perhaps he came while I was in town. I went in for fresh vegetables and bread. Oh, and I met Rose. She took me to their place and gave me some mutton left over from yesterday. She refused to take any money – she said the mutton has to be used up before it goes off.'

'So where did he get to?' Grandpa interrupted, looking around.

'The little rascal,' laughed May. 'He's probably skived off and is lazing around somewhere.'

'Hm. Didn't strike me as the lazy type,' Grandpa grunted, as he dipped his spoon into his stew. We forgot about Mike as we ate the welcoming meal.

As soon as it was dark, John Joe took his leave again.

'Off to see the fine ladies of Ballarat?' sniffed May.

John Joe laughed. 'Nothing so flighty, May,' he said. 'Women don't belong where I'm going.'

'So is it bare-knuckle fighting or something nasty like that, then?' May went on. We'd heard that such sports were held in the seedier parts of the camp, especially near the sly-grog tents.

'There might be fighting involved in time to come,' John Joe answered enigmatically. 'Fighting for justice, that is.' A knowing look passed between him and Grandpa.

Grandpa shook his head. 'There must be a better way,' he began.

'No, Mr Maher,' said John Joe. 'The diggers are meeting.'

'Oh, give it a rest, John Joe,' I put in. 'We've been working so hard, can't we just take it easy? This will all end, you'll see.'

'We'll all see, Esty,' he said, 'soon enough.'

Grandpa went off to smoke his pipe with some of the nearby diggers whom we'd got to know. Most of them had left wives and families in their own countries until they'd made enough money to bring them over to Australia. They teased Grandpa for having three women to look after him – especially Mama with her cooking. I was surprised to see that she had taken up sewing again.

'What are you making?' I asked, when we'd cleared the dishes away.

Mama shook out a short length of fabric. 'A flag,' she replied.

'A flag?' said May, leaning closer to inspect. 'What do you want a flag for, Mrs Maher?.'

'It's a flag for the top of our tent,' said Mama. 'Have you noticed that all the other tents have flags? They have different designs on them, so that the post can be delivered.'

'Are we expecting post, Mama?' I asked. 'Who'd be writing to us?'

Mama smiled, as she bent over her needlework again. 'I've written home,' she said. 'I sent a letter from the Post Office a couple of weeks ago.'

'Did you?' I exclaimed. We hadn't talked about

home much. I suppose we wanted to forget the misery we'd left behind, and we felt guilty because we'd escaped all the horror there.

Mama looked up at me. 'I've written to Mrs Casey because you told me so many times on board ship how good she was to you.'

'But Mama,' I said gently. 'Mrs Casey can't read.'

'I know that, Esty,' Mama replied. 'I've sent it to Mr Egan, your grandpa's friend at the Burgesses. I know he'll take the letter to her and read it. And I know he'll write down her news to send back here to us. So that's why I'm making this flag – to identify us.'

'And what address did you put on top of the letter, Mama? What will they write on the envelope to reach us here?'

Mama smiled and held out the fabric. 'See?' she pointed at a half-finished symbol. 'The bridge on the road to Lord Craythorn's,' she said with pride. 'The bridge you had to cross to get our passage here. Don't you think a bridge is significant? We've crossed the bridge of a whole ocean. So the address I put was *Mahers, Bridge End*, because that's what will be embroidered under the design. And that's what will be on the envelope when a letter comes: *Mahers, Bridge End, Sovereign Hill, Ballarat, Colony of Victoria, Australia*,' she said, holding out the needlework in front of her.

Mrs Casey: memories came flooding back to me and I shivered. I wanted to shut that part of my life away. But if I were to hold on to one memory, it would certainly be Mrs Casey.

'By the way, May,' said Mama. 'Speaking of letters, I have something for you from the Bakers.'

'For me?' said May, her eyes wide with surprise.

Mama picked up her bag and took out a letter. May looked at it for a moment before taking it.

'Go on, May,' I said. 'It won't bite.' I was as curious as she was.

'Why is Rose writing to May?' I asked teasingly.

May put the letter in her pocket and grinned at me. 'It's for me to know and you to find out,' she said.

'Aren't you going to read it, May?' Mama put in. 'It's from Adam,'

May looked from Mama to me. 'In my own good time,' she replied. 'Just because you taught me to read, Esty, doesn't mean you can see my private correspondence.'

Mama and I both laughed.

Grandpa came back and tapped out his pipe on a log.

'Those four English boys,' he chuckled. 'Beans and bread, beans and bread. No wonder they think we're spoiled over here. Your cooking is the envy of the camp, Kate.'

Mama smiled and looked up from her sewing. 'Well, why don't we invite them to supper tomorrow evening?'

'Splendid,' said Grandpa enthusiastically. 'I'll get some money and you can buy an extra bit of mutton – and this time Rose must let you pay. Don't worry,' he went on, as Mama began to protest about the cost.

'There's still money left from our find. We haven't touched the licence fee money.'

He bent down and crept under the wagon to the hidden place where we kept our money box. Mama turned back to her sewing.

We jumped, when Grandpa swore and began to frantically search underneath the wagon, shaking it and tapping the axles.

'What is it, Father?' asked Mama, dropping her sewing. 'What's wrong?'

I could see, even in the firelight, that Grandpa's face was white.

'It's gone,' he said. 'Our money's gone!'

Chapter Twenty-Six

We lit torches and searched the area all around the camp, but there was no sign of our precious box. It was May who spotted the faint bloodstains beside one of the wagon wheels. We looked at one another, stunned. Mike!

'I can't believe he'd do that,' whispered Mama. 'I can't believe Mike would rob us.'

Grandpa eased himself on to a log and covered his face with his hands. 'It's gone,' he said. 'No matter who took it, our money is gone.'

'Maybe if we look further,' I said. 'We could ask…'

Grandpa shook his head. 'No good, lass,' he said. 'I'll go across to the tent he shares with his brother, but I don't hold out much hope. If Mike has stolen it, then he's hardly likely to stay around.'

'I'll come with you,' I said. But Grandpa put out his hand to stop me

'Best if I deal with this alone, Esty. We have to be careful we don't make wrongful accusations.'

'But, Mr Maher,' May butted in. 'There are bloodstains around the wagon. It stands to reason that Mike came to have his cut dressed, found nobody here and helped himself to the money. He must have seen you take money from the box to pay his wages. How else would he know where we keep our cash?'

Grandpa shook his head again and moved away through the maze of tents and huts. Mama, May and I were too shocked to do anything except keep up a search that we knew in our hearts would be fruitless. Finally, Mama eased herself up on to her feet.

'There's no point, girls,' she said. 'The box didn't accidentally fall from its hiding-place and walk away. It was taken.'

The three of us waited silently for Grandpa to come back.

'Maybe Mr Maher has found that lad,' May said eventually. 'Maybe the young thief thought he'd get away with it…'

'No, May,' said Mama wearily. 'If he were clever enough to steal, then he'd be clever enough to get away as far as he could.'

'We'll know soon enough,' I said. 'Here he comes.' I knew by Grandpa's stooped, defeated gait that the news would be bad. He shook his head as he drew near.

'As I thought,' he said, sitting down. 'His brother says he hasn't had sight of him since he left for work this morning.'

'Perhaps he's covering up for him, Grandpa,' I said. 'He could be hiding Mike somewhere…'

'No,' Grandpa put in. 'I believe him, Esty. He's puzzled, just like us. He seems a decent sort and I believe him.'

'Well, I suppose he's not responsible for his brother,'

said Mama. 'Still, family loyalty is a strong thing, Father. People will say anything to protect their own.'

'I'm telling you, Kate,' said Grandpa with a hint of annoyance, 'the boy was telling me the truth. Trust me, I've been long enough on this earth to know the difference between truth and lies.'

'Indeed, Father,' replied Mama gently. 'But you also trusted Mike, didn't you?'

Grandpa gave a sigh. 'I did,' he said. 'And I made a mistake, it seems. Look, why don't we all get some rest? There's little point in pondering this … this catastrophe. Go!' he shouted, when Mama tried to say something.

Mama was visibly shocked, as were May and I. In all my life and through all of our ups and downs here and in Ireland, Grandpa had never once raised his voice like this. Silently, Mama made her way to the tent. May looked as if she wanted to say something, but changed her mind and followed. I looked at Grandpa, his face furrowed in the light of the fire. I wanted so much to comfort him, but what can you offer a man who has just lost everything? So, with a brief backward glance, I followed the others.

'He's not angry with you, Mama,' I said. 'He's just upset with himself. This is the most awful thing that could happen.'

'I know, Esty,' Mama sighed. 'I don't know what's going to happen to us now.'

'Don't worry, Mrs Maher,' said May. 'We found some gold. We'll surely find some more before the next licence fee is due.'

'Thank you, May,' Mama forced a smile. 'That's our only hope. I can't bear to think what will become of us if that fails.'

I was too numb to try and give her an answer. Anyway, there was none to give. I waited until I thought the other two were asleep before stealing out of my bed and picking up my shawl.

'Where are you going, child?'

I froze. 'I'm just going outside for a moment, Mama,' I replied. 'It's so stuffy in here, and I can't sleep.'

'You want to talk to Grandpa, is that it?' Mama whispered. 'Perhaps he's best left alone, Esty. He's angry.'

'It's all right,' I whispered back. 'I'll just see how he is. If he sends me away, I won't argue.'

Grandpa was staring into the fire, his arms resting on his knees, his hands clenching and unclenching. I said nothing, just sat down beside him.

'This is a bad thing, Esty,' he murmured. 'A bad, bad thing.'

'We might find more gold,' I said, echoing May's optimism. 'We still have time, Grandpa.'

He turned to look at me, and I was shocked to see the despair in his eyes. I wanted to hug him and make everything all right – but that was just being childish.

'That's the trouble,' he said, with a slight shake in his voice. 'The Commissioner has stepped up the licence inspection to twice a week.'

'Twice a week!'

Grandpa nodded. 'This is why the miners are

meeting every evening, to protest at the crippling fees and the increasing demands, and the fact that they have no vote and therefore no rights. That's where John Joe goes all the time. He keeps me informed. There's going to be trouble, Esty, and I worry about your safety and your mama and May. And now this…' he gestured towards the wagon. 'It's all hopeless. It's my fault. I should have split the money up into smaller sums and put them in several different hiding places.'

'It's not your fault, Grandpa,' I said. 'How were you to know Mike was a thief?'

Grandpa was shaking his head. 'I didn't know, Esty. How could I have known, or even suspected? You knew the lad. He seemed honest and hard-working – one of our own, an Irish lad.' He shook his head again and looked into the fire. 'Robbed by one of our own.'

A voice cut into our subdued conversation.

'Why are you two up so late?' It was John Joe, guiding his horse into the small compound where we kept both horses. 'It's past midnight.'

Then he sat and faced Grandpa. 'The diggers are getting furious, Mr Maher,' he said. 'Some want immediate action – a full confrontation, but Peter Lalor is insisting on a peaceful protest to get our message across to the authorities. Me, I'd prefer to go in with my fists and *make* them listen to us.' He leaned closer to Grandpa. 'Are you listening, Mr Maher?'

Grandpa raised his eyes wearily and looked at John Joe. 'We're finished, lad,' he said in a low voice. 'We have nothing.'

Chapter Twenty-Seven

Grandpa's anger was nothing compared to John Joe's. When Grandpa told him of our loss, he jumped up in a rage and clenched his fists.

'I'll search for him, Mr Maher,' he said through gritted teeth. 'I'll find him and drag him back. He'll pay for this.'

'Sit down, John Joe,' said Grandpa, as John Joe made a move to get his horse again. 'There's no point. He'll be well gone by now and there's no knowing which direction he's gone in. Besides, it's more important that you're here to work with us. More than ever, we're relying on making a find before that lot come here again for the licence. After that...' He sighed, and gazed into the fire.

We went to the diggings before daybreak the next morning in the hope of making a find. Grandpa had warned us not to mention our loss to anyone. 'There are thieving rascals out there,' he said. 'People who'd be glad of our predicament and try to buy us out for a pittance. We're not giving up yet,' he added grimly.

With every tap of the hammer and with every gravel-washing at the creek, we held our breath. But by late evening there was no find. John Joe wanted to keep on working. He said he'd work through the night, but Grandpa insisted that it was more important to rest.

'You'd be too tired to work tomorrow, lad,' he said. 'We need extra strength right now.'

So we covered our shaft as usual, and went home in silence. We were all in a sober mood that night as we sat down to supper. With three days until the next licence inspection, was this to be one of our last meals here?

John Joe put his elbows on the table and leaned towards Grandpa. 'Mr Maher,' he began. 'I could get work with one of the big mining companies. They pay well and I could earn enough to keep us until…'

'No, John Joe,' said Grandpa. 'Not yet. If no miracle happens before those troops come back, then you can do as you wish. But for now, we must continue as we are.'

'It's just as well we didn't invite those nice English diggers over for supper,' said May. 'We would have been in no mood for their company.'

Her remark sparked something in my mind.

'That's it!' I exclaimed. 'Mama's stew!'

'What's wrong with my stew?' asked Mama, as I wiped my mouth.

'Nothing at all,' I replied. 'That's the whole point. Your stew is perfect, Mama. So perfect, that every digger wants some.'

'I don't see,' began Grandpa.

'Oh, but I do.' Mama smiled as she realised what I meant. 'Esty's suggesting that I sell my stews. Isn't that it, Esty?'

'Yes,' I said. 'Think about it. Those hungry diggers – especially the ones who are doing well – would be delighted to pay for good food. You've heard what they say about the smell of Mama's cooking.'

'She's right, Mr Maher,' agreed May. 'We could prepare the vegetables the night before. It wouldn't be hard work – we'd only be sitting by the fire anyway, so we might as well be doing something useful. All Mrs Maher would have to do the next day is to cook them.'

'I have enough money left in my purse to buy vegetables,' said Mama. 'And maybe a little meat – which I can cut up very fine.'

'What about plates?' put in John Joe.

'We'll ask them to bring their own,' replied May.

'I'm not sure about this,' Grandpa began doubtfully.

'Oh, but I am,' said Mama. 'We could make good money by boiling up a few vegetables and mutton.'

'It's too much work for you,' said Grandpa.

Mama put her hands on her hips. 'Too much work, is it?' she said, leaning closer to Grandpa. 'Father, I spent months making cauldrons of soup to feed those starving people back home when food was scarce. Don't you think I could feed a crowd of diggers here, where ingredients are plentiful?'

Grandpa was taken aback. 'I suppose so,' he said.

And so we plotted and planned well into the night. I'd never seen Mama so animated. Perhaps it was that she felt she could use her skills to save us. She'd always been subservient both to Papa and Grandpa, and now here she was, taking on a real business. She beamed at me and said, 'We'll make this do well, Esty.'

It's a funny thing about life: one moment you can be in the depths of despair – the next, you're working out a new plan to make things better.

The next day was Sunday. Grandpa and John Joe went to the shaft on their own, even though working on the Sabbath was frowned upon. May and I went into Ballarat to buy vegetables. Mama took the wagon and went to visit the Bakers.

'Perhaps they'll have some left-over bones,' she said. 'They'd add flavour and substance to the broth.'

Despite our plight, May and I giggled with excitement as we made our way through the town. There were some diggers hanging about the bowling saloon, and they whistled at us as we passed.

'Don't look back, Esty,' May said. 'That only encourages them.'

'Perhaps I want to.'

'That's common, and not nice,' said May, glancing back.

'La-de-da,' I laughed, poking her in the ribs.

As we crossed to the grocery store, we met a group of troops on the street. May pulled me on to the verandah outside the store as they passed. My heart skipped a beat when I recognised the young trooper from the hotel. He recognised me, too, and we stared for a moment that seemed forever. He's nothing, I said to myself after they'd gone. He's just like the rest of those upstarts in their red uniforms, and I want nothing to do with him.

But still I looked back in his direction as May drew me into the store.

Mama was excited when she got back.

'We're so lucky,' she said excitedly. 'Not only did the Bakers give me two fine legs of mutton, but Rose has said she wants to help. She's bringing her own large pot, so we'll have two fires and two pots going. Isn't that wonderful?'

That evening Mama, May, Grandpa and I wrote out handbills for John Joe to put up.

'*Come to the Bridge End sign*', it said. '*Sample Mama Maher's Excellent Stew for sixpence. Bring your own plate.*'

By ten o'clock we were exhausted. We looked at the mountain of vegetables we'd prepared.

'What if nobody comes?' said May.

'Of course they'll come,' I said. 'Wouldn't you, if you were a hungry digger?'

The next morning we went to work as usual – Grandpa, John Joe, May and I. Even though we'd prepared ourselves, we were heavy with disappointment when our dig yielded nothing. As we closed our shaft for the night, we tried not to dwell on what would happen if our great plan didn't work out.

'What'll we do if nobody…?'

'Shush, May,' I said. 'Let's not even think of it.'

Sure enough, when we got to our tent, the only people there were Mama and Rose. The smell was enticing, but any pleasure we had was cancelled out by the awful thought that nobody would want any of the stew. We washed, and changed our clothes.

'We'd better feed ourselves first,' said Rose, ever the practical one. 'No point in standing by with our tummies rumbling. Come on, everyone, sit down and have some of this beautiful broth.'

'This is very good of you, Rose,' said Grandpa, holding out his plate. 'But aren't you needed by James and Adam?'

'Ha!' laughed Rose, waving the ladle to drive home her point. 'The shambles is finished, the sheep are out to grass and we've enough mutton in the meat safe for two days – no point in keeping any more to go bad and smelly. All I'd be doing is nagging at those two men of mine. It's much better here. Besides, it's good to be among my friends again.' She winked at May. She had brought her another letter.

Mama kept glancing around anxiously. 'No sign of anyone yet.'

'Calm down, Kate,' said Rose. 'Give them time to clean up. No self-respecting miner is going to bring his dust and grime to table.'

'I beg to differ, Ma'am,' laughed John Joe. 'Some of the miners I've met would come covered in a week's mud…'

'Will you shush, John Joe,' May said, pointing her spoon at him. 'Keep your daft words to yourself.'

But I could see that Mama was upset by his remark. She looked doubtfully at the two simmering pots.

'Look!' said Grandpa. 'I believe we have company.' Sure enough, two diggers had appeared from behind our wagon. They stopped, when they saw us sitting at the table. Grandpa got up and beckoned them over.

'Have you come for some of Mama Maher's excellent stew?' he asked. 'Here, sit down,' he went on, indicating the rough bench he and John Joe had made shortly after we'd arrived. Shyly the two diggers sat down at the table and nodded at us.

'Up, Esty,' said May, giving me a nudge. 'We can't be sitting down when there are customers to serve.'

We took their plates to Mama and Rose, who filled them with steaming broth.

'Well, that's one shilling earned,' May whispered to me.

'Is there anything I can do?' asked Grandpa.

'Yes,' replied Rose. 'Get out of our way, you and the lad. Too many of us dancing attendance would make our customers nervous.'

'True,' said John Joe. 'You come with me, Mr Maher. It's time you met some of my friends.'

'What if a row breaks out?' asked Grandpa. 'There could be some very rough elements here.'

'A row?' said Rose, waving the ladle again. 'Don't you worry. I know how to deal with anyone who dares to even hint at trouble. You can rest assured of that.'

Grandpa looked helplessly at Mama, but she simply nodded.

'Do go, Father,' she said. 'It's time you got acquainted with other people.'

'More customers!' said May.

And so there were. Many more. Most of them were, like Grandpa's English friends, working to make enough to bring their families here. But a few brought along their wives. Soon we were so busy that we could scarcely keep up. There were too many to sit at our small table, so they took their plates and sat under the nearby trees, or settled cross-legged on the ground. They were noisy and good-humoured. May, who had declared herself in charge of finance, took their sixpences before the plates were filled.

'That way, there can be no cheating,' said Rose.

At one stage, May showed me the bag bulging with money. She folded her apron up over the bag and tied the ends around her waist. As we cleared up, after turning away several latecomers who'd arrived after the last servings had been scraped from the pots, May's movements were accompanied by jingling coins.

The four of us stretched out under the tree exhausted, though it didn't stop me writing in my journal.

'Shouldn't we count the money?' asked Mama.

'No, Mrs Maher,' said May, putting her hands protectively over the bundle of coins. 'This does not leave my person until Mr Maher finds a safe place for it. There could be someone watching who'd pounce if I untie it. If they want the money, they'll have to take me as well.'

'They wouldn't dare, May,' said Mama. 'You'd terrify them.'

Drunk with our success, we couldn't stop laughing.

Chapter Twenty-Eight

For the next three evenings, the pattern was the same. Word had spread, and soon there were queues from our tent almost down to the first diggings. Mama and Rose stocked up with even more vegetables and two more large pots. Rose would not hear of Mama paying for the mutton with the money we'd earned.

'No,' she insisted. 'That money must be used for your licence, otherwise the whole effort will have been for nothing. I've told you, Kate, you can pay us back when you're back on your feet. We're quite comfortably off, me and my two men. We sold our farm and part of our stock to get here. What we have is our own – and our meat stall is making good money every day.'

The letters to and from May and Adam via Rose continued to brighten our evenings. Although I didn't actually read them, May told me as much as she felt I should know. It was a pity that Adam couldn't visit us himself.

'In good time,' she said, when I mentioned it. 'He and his father work late, Esty. Then they take turns minding the stall and the stock. There are thieves out there who'd steal the eye out of your head.'

She broke off. We knew all about thieves.

'Anyway,' she went on. 'It will be different when they set up a proper business in town.'

'And John Joe?' I said. 'How will you break this to John Joe?' I was still worried that he'd be hurt, though he'd scarcely shown any attention to May – he was so involved in the miners' affairs.

May shrugged. 'I'll find a way to tell him, when the time is right.'

One evening, long after the last digger had left, and Rose had gone home, Mama was relaxing with her sewing, May was snoozing under a tree and I was writing my journal by the light of a lantern. Suddenly, there was Grandpa, and a distinguished-looking gentleman with him.

'I'd like to present Mr Henry Seekamp,' said Grandpa. 'Mr Seekamp owns and edits *The Ballarat Times*. He's very sympathetic to us diggers, and isn't afraid to say so in his paper. He's married to a woman from Dublin, so he's used to our accent!'

I made room for them to sit down, and took my lantern over to sit near May. I half-listened to the droning conversation at the table. It seemed to be the usual talk of injustice, crippling fees and the miners' unrest, so I concentrated on my writing.

'I don't know where you get your energy, Esty Maher,' muttered May drowsily. 'I'm so tired, what with the mining and serving dinners, that I think my legs have worn away up to my knees. I'm afraid to look down in case my feet are missing.'

'That's what I love about you, May,' I chuckled, as I smoothed a new page. 'You've always made me laugh. I scarcely had a sense of humour before I met you and your rag rugs.'

'Get away with you,' May muttered, turning over for another snooze. It was quite true, I thought. As an only child in a house of adults, there had not been much of the nonsense and silliness that makes one's tummy shake with laughter.

When he was about to go, Mr Seekamp looked towards me.

'What are you writing?' he asked.

Mama laughed. 'She's writing her journal. Any spare time she has – and that's precious little – Esty is either reading or writing.'

I shuffled around a bit, embarrassed at being singled out by this gentleman. Especially when he came towards me.

'What sort of things do you write?' he asked.

'Just things about the camp,' I replied. 'The everyday things that I see here.'

'May I see?' he asked.

I covered my journal with my hand. 'I don't think it would interest you,' I began. 'It's very ordinary.'

'Go on, Esty,' Grandpa said encouragingly. 'Let the man have a look.'

Reluctantly, I passed Mr Seekamp my precious journal, hoping that he couldn't see my blushes in the light of the lantern. He flipped through my work, pausing every now and then to peer at something that caught his attention.

'This is very well written, young lady,' he said eventually. 'How would you like to try writing a short article for my paper? Nothing too taxing,' he added, when he noted my confusion. 'Just a brief article about life here on the diggings. You are just the person to write it, because you are right here in the thick of the workings. I'll pay you two shillings. Will you consider it?'

For once in my life, I was struck dumb.

'Go on, Esty,' May urged, suddenly wide awake. 'She's good at writing,' she went on, looking up at Mr Seekamp.

'It's a splendid idea,' said Grandpa. 'Do say yes, Esty. You know you want to be a writer. Now is your chance to make a start.'

I could see Mama's face filled with pride. I looked back at Mr Seekamp to see if he was really serious. He was.

'All right,' I said. 'But if it's no good, you must tell me at once.'

And so it was decided that I would write a short article on life in the chaotic world of the goldfield. As Mr Seekamp took his leave, I turned to May.

'What on earth will I write about?' I asked.

'Oh, you'll think of something, Esty,' laughed May. 'You always do.'

'I won't,' I groaned. 'Now that I've been asked to write something that people will read, I just won't be able to do it. It's different from writing for myself. I'll die.'

'No you won't,' retorted May. 'You'll earn that two shillings and that's it. I'll help.'

'Will you?'

'Not with the writing,' May laughed. 'But I'll keep my ears open for any gossip.'

I laughed too, mostly because any gossip May heard, I would hear too, since we went everywhere together.

However it was May who provided the first bit of news. It was early October. We were now several weeks into our Mama Maher's Stew business and all was going well. We always managed to pay our licence fee, and though the long working day was fatiguing, we were so happy to be still here that we ignored our aching limbs.

That evening the diggers seemed restless. There was much subdued muttering. I was stirring a pot of stew on the fire when May rushed over.

'Have you heard?' she said.

'Heard what, May?'

'A young digger was shot last night at the Eureka Hotel.'

The Eureka Hotel was a place where the military drank at night. It was a place most diggers avoided, preferring instead to be with their own at the sly-grog tents.

'Was he badly hurt?' I asked, still stirring. We'd become quite used to diggers wounding one another with guns or knives or fists.

'He's dead,' said May in a hushed voice. 'The diggers are furious.'

'Dead?' I asked, stopping mid-stir. 'Who did that?'

May looked about her and leaned closer. 'They're saying it was the owner who shot him. This could turn nasty, if we're to believe the diggers.'

'There's been talk of things turning nasty for some time now, May,' I said. 'I'm sure it will all blow over.'

But it didn't blow over. Even Grandpa, who preferred to stay outside the plotting and scheming of disgruntled diggers, was showing signs of frustration that turned to anger later on, when the publican who shot the young digger was found not guilty by a magistrate who just happened to be the publican's friend.

'This is it,' Grandpa said, on the evening of the trial. 'This corruption of justice will spark off something terrible.'

His words were to become reality sooner than we expected. When John Joe set off on his usual nightly jaunt later, Grandpa tried to stop him.

'Don't go, lad,' he said, putting out a restraining hand. 'Let those who would, deal with this. It's not our fight.'

'I'm afraid it is, Mr Maher,' said John Joe, pulling away. 'Haven't we had enough injustice at home, without having to deal with it here?'

Grandpa sighed and sank on to the bench. Mama said nothing.

'Mr Maher is right, John Joe,' May said gently. 'Listen to him.'

John Joe took us all in as we looked at him, pleading. 'I'm part of this,' he said. 'I must go.'

Grandpa suddenly seemed older. He gave one last despairing look at John Joe.

'No matter what happens tonight,' he said to Mama, May and me, 'you must stay in the tent. Things are bubbling up to a dangerous level and there's no turning back.'

We were too scared to ask what he meant, or perhaps we didn't want to know, so we retired quietly to our tent.

'Esty,' May whispered to me later. 'What do you think will happen?'

'I don't know, May,' I replied. 'I don't really know what's going on, but it sounds serious.'

Later, we heard shouting that spread like a rising wave all around the camp. There were loud voices close by. Pausing only to pull on our boots and throw our shawls around our shoulders, Mama, May and I ventured out. Others were coming out of their tents, as puzzled as we were.

Then someone shouted.

'Fire!'

Sure enough, in the distance, flames were rising into the sky.

'Dear God!' exclaimed Mama, looking around desperately. There was no sign of Grandpa.

'It's the Eureka Hotel!' someone shouted. 'They've set fire to the Eureka!'

They? Did that include John Joe?

Mama came closer to me and clutched my arm. 'I've no doubt that John Joe is in on this,' she said, as if reading my mind. 'But where's your grandpa?'

'You know Grandpa,' I said, patting her hand. 'He'll be all right. Grandpa doesn't do dangerous things.'

We all jumped at the sound of shots.

'The police,' someone said. 'It's the police!'

'Oh, God,' said May, her hands to her face. 'If John Joe is part of this, I'll kill him.' Then she realised what she'd said and shook her head. 'If the police don't kill him first.'

Chapter Twenty-Nine

People were racing past in confusion. Mama said it was important that we three stay together.

'With all this going on,' she shouted above the clamour, 'there could be some whose intentions are less than honourable, people who would take advantage of the situation.'

'Well, at least our money is safe now,' whispered May. And so it was. And so was the next lump of gold that Grandpa found. It wasn't much, just slightly larger than our first find, but our excitement was somewhat dampened by events going on around us. John Joe said it would be better to hold on to the gold until things settled. So he and Grandpa buried our dinner money and the gold in the ground under our bedding. We weren't taking any chances.

We felt safer inside our tent. But the noise continued with frightening intensity until I could bear it no more. I got up and grabbed my shawl.

'Where are you going, Esty?' asked May

'I'm just going to have a look,' I replied.

'Please, Esty,' said Mama. 'It's too dangerous.'

'I can't just sit here, Mama,' I cried. 'I have to know

where Grandpa and John Joe are.'

Before she could say anything else, I slipped out of the tent. Although the shouting had subsided, there were still diggers rushing past, their faces looking troubled in the light of the lanterns they carried. I was caught up in the running, and carried along towards the scene of the fire. Everyone came to a stop a short distance from the inferno. Flames were shooting from the windows of the hotel, sparks flying into the night sky like an explosion of orange stars. By now the police had arrived, some of them mounted, and they were trying to round up the nearest diggers. Their silhouettes were terrifying, as they charged about with batons, hitting out at anyone in sight.

'Keep back!' someone shouted.

The crowd shrank back, some falling over with the force of the bodies. Half-running and half-falling, I tried to push my way back. I could hear the thudding hooves of horses behind me. Someone grabbed my arm and pulled me into the crowd. I recognised a digger who was one of our customers.

'Don't look back!' he yelled, pulling me roughly.

But of course I did glance back, and was just in time to see Grandpa among the stragglers. With a heave, I pulled away from my rescuer and ran back towards Grandpa. His face was contorted with pain.

'Grandpa!' I screamed.

As I ran towards him, a mounted policeman galloped towards us. He stooped down to strike Grandpa. But another rider cut across his path and allowed us to run into the crowd. When I looked back I saw, in the light from the blazing building, that the rider who'd helped us get away was the young trooper from the hotel. He gave me a brief nod and rode away.

Grandpa and I held on to each other as we were swept along by the retreating diggers. When we reached the safety of the tents, we felt more at ease. The mounted police would not risk their horses by galloping in the dark over land pitted with mine shafts.

'Esty, lass,' he gasped, pausing to catch his breath. 'What were you doing? I told you…'

'I know what you told me, Grandpa. But how could I sit in our tent knowing you were out here? Besides, if I hadn't turned up when I did, you'd probably have been dragged off to jail.' I didn't add that it was my young trooper who'd come between Grandpa and his would-be captor. I hoped the trooper wouldn't get into trouble, though the instant was so fleeting that I believed his action would be considered just part of the general mayhem. The look he'd given me gave me a warm feeling inside.

Grandpa smiled. 'Is there anyone born who can control you?'

'No, Grandpa,' I laughed.

Mama was all fuss and bother when we got back. Grandpa gently shushed her questions.

'It's all right, Kate,' he said, lowering himself on to the bench. May had stirred up the fire again and was looking anxiously at the faces as they passed. 'We're safe,' Grandpa added. 'Let's rest a while, eh?'

Mama looked worried. But her anxiety was cut short by the arrival of John Joe. His face was blackened and he was out of breath. May went over and put her hands on his shoulders.

'Are you all right, John Joe?' she asked.

He nodded, and sat beside Grandpa.

'It was a close call,' he muttered.

'Were you one of the…?' May began, but Grandpa caught her eye and shook his head. I knew what that meant. Whatever John Joe had been up to, it was best if we didn't know about it. Then, if questions were asked, as no doubt they would, we would know nothing.

'There's no turning back,' John Joe said later, as we sipped tea. 'All hell will break loose now.'

He said it in a tone of satisfaction. But what could be good about the promise of more violence?

Chapter Thirty

Sure enough, shortly afterwards we heard that the Commissioner had requested reinforcements of British soldiers from Melbourne. They would arrive soon. The diggers were fearful and angry. Despite my original resolve not to become embroiled in their grievances, I found myself listening to the diggers around us and making notes in my journal. Not only that but, ignoring Mama's concern, I went along to the meetings before the reinforcements arrived. Grandpa came with me. I was surprised at the number of women who also came along and raised their voices.

'All we want,' Peter Lalor said, holding up his hands for calm. 'All we want is fair representation and the abolition of the licence tax.'

'Fair enough,' Grandpa whispered to me. 'If we diggers had a vote, then matters would be dealt with in a civilised manner. Why can't the powers-that-be realise that?'

As May and I travelled back and forth from mine shaft to creek, I also listened to what the diggers were saying up on Sovereign Hill. I listened to them as we served them stew in the evenings. And I knew that despite Peter Lalor's call for restraint, many were now too angry to be peaceful.

'Will there be more trouble, Esty?' May asked me one evening, as we cleaned up. 'Do you think all of this will end in a bloody battle?'

I shrugged my shoulders. It frightened me to see that Grandpa was now as involved as John Joe. I knew he would normally shun anything that might end in violence, but his sympathies were with the miners. As I wrote, I couldn't help wondering what would happen if all our hard work and dreams were to dissolve in war between the military and the diggers. What would become of us? We would lose everything

'May,' I said one night, 'Do you think we should have stayed in service? All those nights when we looked at the pictures of the Australian goldfields in *The Illustrated London News* and I told you about the gold – do you think I was living a dream? You'd be safe if you'd stayed with the Burgesses.'

'Will you shush,' May said, pulling me close. 'This country is – how can I say it, Esty? It's more than I could have imagined. You've opened my life, Esty Maher, opened up a whole world beyond that stuffy estate back home. I love this country, and I'll cope with whatever life sends us. And so will you. We're here, we're alive and we're going to stick together through thick and thin. We're as good as – no, better even, than a family – you, me, your mam, your grandpa and John Joe. So, no more of your daft doubts.'

I took some comfort from her optimism, but

underneath I feared the outcome of the miners' simmering rage. The nightly meetings grew bigger as more and more diggers gathered to air their grievances. Along with Peter Lalor and other rational people, Grandpa tried to calm the frustrated men, but they'd become too angry to listen to reason any more.

And I felt myself siding with them. Many of these men had come from the other side of the world and had invested all they had in the goldfields. If they didn't keep up with the crippling licence fees, they were doomed to penury – just like ourselves. All that money going to England. It didn't seem fair.

'It's not just the licence fee, Esty,' Grandpa said to me one evening, as I was writing my journal. 'It's to do with our rights. There are some blackguards among us who are up to all kinds of mischief, but that's no reason for all of us to be treated as criminals. Most are like ourselves – good people who have come to this new country in search of a decent living. All we want is to be treated with respect and have the right to vote – to have our say.'

Matters came to a head one night in November. Grandpa told me that something big was about to happen as we set out to a place called Bakery Hill. I was amazed at the number of diggers massed there. A big flagpole was erected and, in an act of defiance after several heated speeches, the diggers burnt their licences. I gasped. I couldn't believe they'd do such a foolhardy thing.

'What will happen now?' I whispered to Grandpa.

He squeezed my arm. 'I don't know, Esty lass,' he sighed. 'I just don't know. But, for better or for worse, there's no turning back now.'

Amidst loud cheers, a flag was raised. It fluttered up the flagpole and caught the breeze at the top. In the light of the many lanterns I could see the design as it billowed in the night breeze.

'The Southern Cross!' I exclaimed. 'It's the Southern Cross!'

'It is,' said Grandpa. 'The stars of the Southern Cross – the symbol of the miners.'

Peter Lalor stood under the flag and voiced the now-familiar requests of the miners. Fair representation, abolition of the licence tax and votes for all were the main demands, just as Grandpa had told me. That sounded reasonable. I couldn't understand why these requests would provoke such a reaction from the authorities. After his speech, Peter Lalor swore allegiance to the Southern Cross and, with one voice, so did every miner at the gathering, including Grandpa.

Then he too burnt his licence. 'The die is cast, Esty,' he said.

Chapter Thirty-One

Friday, 1st December dawned with a promise of sweltering heat. I felt I'd never get accustomed to the upside-down seasons here in Australia.

'December,' May said to me later, as we fought off the flies that even managed to squeeze under our veils. 'At home we'd be scraping the frost off the windows in our attic, Esty. Don't you remember? Pulling back the blankets while it was still dark to face another day pandering to Miss Emma and her ma. And the cold! God, I can still remember the cold in that Big House. So cold that your fingers would be numb. I used to envy the kitchen maids down there in the heat of the big stove.'

'Oh, frost, beautiful frost,' I gasped. 'What I'd give for just a handful of that frost right now.'

'And Christmas,' May went on. 'Mrs Casey would be making the puddings.' she added. 'And cakes. She made the best Christmas cakes in Ireland. She told me so herself. She'd be soaking the fruit in brandy and smacking the hands of anyone she'd catch taking a handful.'

'I wasn't there in the days of plenty,' I reminded her.

'I came during the Hunger, remember?'

We fell silent.

There was an undercurrent of excitement around the diggings that morning – a feeling of something about to happen. As we took our barrow to the creek, May looked around with a frown.

'Is it my imagination, or are there fewer workers around?' she asked.

'It's your imagination,' I laughed.

'No, May's right,' said John Joe, his bare torso glistening with sweat. 'Lots of the diggers have gone off to the stockade.'

'What's a stockade?' asked May.

'A big fence made of spiked stakes to protect us from the military,' said John Joe. 'We're expecting trouble.'

'Pah! We're always expecting trouble,' May retorted. 'What's so different about now?'

John Joe just shook his head as he started to work on the gravel we'd brought. His silence frightened me. As we made our way back towards the digging, I too, noticed the absence of many of the miners.

'They're building a fence thing, Mr Maher,' May said to Grandpa, who'd come up to the surface of the shaft for some fresh air and a puff on his pipe. 'John Joe says there's more trouble. Always trouble. You'd think they'd all be fed up with trouble by now, and just get on with things.'

Grandpa gave me a worried look. 'A stockade,' he muttered, giving a great sigh. 'A useless gesture against the might of the Crown.'

I'd wanted him to say something more comforting. But that was just me seeking the reassurance I'd always got from him.

That evening, a great many customers for Mama's stew were missing. The talk among those who had come was of the stockade.

'Let them try their dirty tricks now, those militia men,' someone said. 'We'll be ready for them.'

'Listen to them,' whispered May. 'Like small boys playing war games, they are.'

Away from the firelight, I could see Grandpa and John Joe talking earnestly. Then John Joe went towards the wagon. Was he leaving?

'What are you doing, John Joe?' I asked. 'Are you taking the wagon? Are you going somewhere?'

John Joe smiled. 'I'm going to have a sleep, Esty,' he said.

A sleep? That was not like John Joe. He could go for days without a proper night's sleep and still be full of energy. I felt that the whole order of life had been stirred into an unreal blend of fact and fantasy, and I could make no sense of any of it. Grandpa went over and sat under a tree. I sensed that he wanted to be alone, so I tried to concentrate on cleaning the stew-pots.

We were surprised and delighted later on when Adam turned up unexpectedly in his cart. May blushed, and almost spilled her precious bag of sixpences in her attempt to get her apron off.

'Adam,' said his mother, as surprised as the rest of us. 'What are you doing here? How is Father managing…?'

'It's all right, Ma,' he replied, jumping from the cart. 'A couple of customers are helping watch the sheep.' He went over to May and, like a true gentleman, kissed her hand. Here we were in the midst of impending violence, and May's beau was coming to court her!

John Joe appeared from inside the wagon. I expected some awkwardness, but he simply nodded to Adam.

'Adam,' he said.

Rose laughed. 'Come to see his lady love,' she said, in her usual forthright way.

'Not quite, Ma,' said Adam, going around to the back of the cart. I gasped, when he produced his rifle. What was this all about? I'd read about lovers fighting over their sweethearts – surely this was not about to happen!

But Adam simply handed John Joe the gun.

'Take it,' he said. 'You're better with this than I am. I know what might be ahead and I want you to have it.'

John Joe took the gun. The sight of that terrible weapon in his hands made me gasp.

'No!' I cried out. 'John Joe, don't…'

John Joe looked at me. 'It's all right, Esty,' he said. 'It's just to scare the enemy. A few shots in the air will be enough to frighten them off.'

May had her hands to her face, her eyes wide with fear. 'What are you doing, Adam?' she said. 'Do you want John Joe to be hanged for shooting at the military?'

'No,' replied Adam.

'Thank God,' Rose murmured. 'At least you won't be using it yourself.'

'No, Ma,' said Adam. Then he reached back into the cart and took out a billhook. 'I'll make do with this.'

'Adam!' began Rose. 'This is the miners' fight, lad. Let those who are involved deal with it.'

'I am involved, Ma,' replied Adam. 'All of us here are involved. Whatever happens here in Ballarat affects my life too.' Then he looked at John Joe. 'Are we ready?' he asked.

Mama put her hand on Grandpa's arm. 'Stop them, Father!' she said. Grandpa gently lifted her hand away.

'There's no stopping it now,' he said.

'Foolhardy!' exclaimed Rose, wringing her hands. 'What chance have a few miners against trained troops?'

Without looking back, John Joe and Adam went off together. May clutched my hand. Mama and Rose drew closer together and Mama looked at me, her face tense.

There was nothing I could say to comfort her.

Chapter Thirty-Two

There was little work done at the diggings the following day. Every man seemed to be down at the stockade, including John Joe and Adam. Now and then someone would pass by with word that the miners there were poised at the defence, but that the military were showing no signs of attacking.

'Thank goodness,' said Mama. 'Now perhaps they'll all see how futile this is and it will end.'

Grandpa went down to see for himself how things were progressing. He came back late that night.

'What's happening?' Mama asked. 'Will there be violence, Father?'

Grandpa shook his head. 'Most of the men have gone home,' he said. 'Tomorrow is Sunday. There will be no violence on the Sabbath.'

'So, where's John Joe?' I asked. 'And Adam?'

Grandpa held his hands towards the dying fire. 'Some of the men are staying on,' he replied.

'They're daft,' put in May. 'What's the point of staying in that dismal place if nothing is going to happen?'

Grandpa shrugged. 'They're young,' he said. 'Who can argue with the passion of young men?'

'Do you know something, Esty?' May said to me later as we prepared for bed. 'I used to think that men knew everything, that they were the ones who made all the right decisions and made life easier for us women. But, do you know what I think now?'

'What do you think, May?' I said wearily.

'I think they're mad. All of them. Mad. I think I'll be a nun, all nice and safe in a convent with nothing to do except say lots of Hail Marys, sew silky vestments for bishops, and grow vegetables. Do you think they have convents in this country? I'm sure they'd be delighted to have a fine girl like me.'

I had to laugh. 'May,' I said. 'You wouldn't last five minutes in a convent. You'd give cheek to the Reverend Mother, talk during meals and complain about the lack of men. Now, please let me get on with earning that two shillings from Henry Seekamp.'

'You might not need it,' May whispered, nodding towards Mama's bed, under which lay our money and gold nugget.

'Oh, get some sleep, May,' I said. 'No point in speculating about might or might not.'

Later that night, I was awakened by May shaking my shoulder. 'I can't sleep,' she whispered.

'Well I can,' I replied drowsily. 'Tomorrow is Sunday, and Grandpa said there would be no unpleasantness from the military on a Sunday. They'll all go home tomorrow, those men at the stockade. Now, go back to sleep.'

But she shook me again a few minutes later. 'Let's go down there, Esty.'

'Down where, May? What are you talking about? Look,' – I pointed to the fading darkness through the open flap above our heads – 'It will soon be dawn.'

'I know,' she said. 'But what's the harm in just going down to look? Before they take away the stockade, why not just take a peep and see what it's like?'

By now I was wide awake, and I knew May had no intention of going back to sleep. Besides, I was curious, and if I saw the stockade, I could write a description of it.

'Just a quick look, then,' I whispered. Mama was still asleep, snoring gently. We dressed silently and went out. We didn't take a lantern as we didn't want to draw attention to ourselves. I glanced into the wagon. Grandpa wasn't there. I suppose I'd known that he would follow the boys. Holding hands, we strained to see the path in the pre-dawn, now and then giggling when one of us stumbled.

'Hush!' a sharp voice hissed from dark, thick shrubs ahead of us. May and I clutched one another.

'Who … who's there?' I asked. The shrubs moved and a stout woman emerged, followed by three or four more. We could barely see their shapes against the sky.

'What are you two doing here?' The stout woman peered at us. 'Come for fun, have you?'

'Certainly not,' May retorted. 'How dare you…'

'We have family in the stockade,' I put in. It was a harmless lie that gained us their sympathy. At once their attitude changed and they beckoned us to join them.

As we stepped towards them, we stopped and gasped.

There, below us, was the infamous stockade. From the lights of the fires and lanterns, we could see that it was less than an acre in size, made up of chopped-down trees, overturned carts, flimsy-looking stakes and slabs of stone. There were lights on in some of the tents. Now and then we'd see shadowy figures moving between the carts and shady hillocks, and hear voices that travelled eerily to where we stood.

Beyond the stockade, a little higher up, there were the tents and houses of the police, military and Government officials. It looked peaceful enough.

'This is it, then, is it?' May whispered. 'The stockade.'

'Indeed it is,' replied one of the women wearily. 'The Eureka Stockade. Some of us here sewed the flag of the Southern Cross.'

'Have you family down there?' I asked.

'My son,' another woman replied. 'And some of us have husbands and brothers.'

Now more women began to emerge. 'We've taken them food,' one of them said. 'And we're waiting.'

Waiting for what? I didn't dare ask.

'I can't see many miners,' May put in, bending forward in the gloom.

'Maybe one hundred or so. Most went home earlier in the night,' the stout woman explained. 'They've taken the Sabbath to be with their families before...' she broke off.

'They'll be back,' someone else said. 'By Sunday evening they'll all be back to show strength of numbers.'

'Sit with us,' said the stout woman, whose name was Hannah. 'Sit on the rug. There's not much we can do, but we'd rather be here than in our tents worrying.'

There was something comforting about being in the company of these women, sharing our anxieties with them. They passed around scones and bread left over from the baskets they'd taken to the miners.

'I wish I knew where John Joe and Adam are,' said May, peering out again.

'Brothers?' someone asked.

'Sweethearts,' I said.

'Esty!' exclaimed May.

'It's true,' I laughed. 'One man is not enough for May. She has two courting her.'

The women laughed. One of them patted May's arm. 'Take the one with money,' she said.

'No,' another put in. 'Choose the gentler one. A gentle man is worth all the gold in Ballarat.'

'And where would you find a gentle digger?' said a voice.

Our laughter was cut short by a cry from one of the women.

'They're coming!' she cried. 'Look.'

We all got up and looked towards the stockade. Sure enough, we could see the troops moving towards the stockade. Behind them came mounted figures brandishing swords that glinted in the firelight. We stood frozen with disbelief, until one of the women began to run down towards the stockade.

'Wake up!' she was shouting. 'They're coming! Get up!'

We watched her until she reached the edge of the stockade, still shouting. Hannah held out her brawny arms to stop the rest of us from following.

'There's nothing we can do,' she said. 'Our men would only try to protect us. We must let them fight unhampered.'

'I'm going back to the diggings to tell them,' someone cried out. 'To get help.'

'I'll come with you,' said May. She looked at me guiltily. 'I can't stay and watch this, Esty! Come with me.'

Part of me wanted to flee from this awful scene, but I knew I must stand firm with these brave women.

'No, May. Go!'

Now the shouting had begun below us. In the faint dawn light I saw someone stand beside the Eureka flag. I could hear his cries as he shouted to the miners to hold their fire, to save their ammunition until the attackers came closer. I knew that voice, I'd heard it often enough at the meetings – it was Peter Lalor. Then he suddenly fell as a shot rang out. And then the shooting really began. We women clutched one another, crying out as more and more people fell. By now the stockade was overrun with soldiers, mounted and on foot, shooting as they advanced.

'Dear God!' sobbed Hannah. 'This is slaughter.'

One or two of the women broke away and ran

towards the battle. Hannah shouted at them to come back, but they were intent only on reaching whoever belonged to them. Someone put her arm around me when I was sick in the bushes.

'It's now we need our strength,' she said, as she wiped my mouth.

She was right. In a few horror-filled minutes the battle was over.

With Hannah leading, we ran to the stockade.

'Shout "Dead!"' Hannah called out to us, just before we climbed over the barricade. I was to find out soon enough what she meant as we approached the injured, groaning miners. The soldiers were shouting at us to go away. Indeed, some of the mounted police were running down any uninjured men they saw trying to escape. But we kept on going, to tend the wounded. By now it was bright enough to see the carnage that had been caused.

Nothing, I thought, is worth this. I stopped to comfort a wounded miner. I knew him – he was one of our dinner men.

'It went through my arm,' he said. 'The bullet just went right through. I'm all right, Esty. Go to someone who's bad.'

'I'll come back later,' I said. There was confusion everywhere. I saw one of the women from the hill sitting with a wounded man in her arms. A soldier with a bayonet approached her.

'Out of the way,' he barked.

'He's dead!' she cried, putting her hand over

the man's face. But he wasn't dead. After the soldier had passed, the man whispered his thanks to the woman. So this was Hannah's plan, I thought. The so-called 'dead' would be claimed by their own and taken away on carts to safety. Now the cry could be heard all around the stockade. 'Dead … dead.' I looked around frantically for Grandpa, and was just in time to see him being marched away with other survivors, including a limping Adam.

'Grandpa!' I screamed, running towards the walking wounded. He turned and waved me away. I knew I'd only cause further trouble – there was nothing I could do but watch the straggling miners being herded towards the military camp. At least he and Adam are alive, I told myself, before turning my attention back to the wounded.

At the foot of the flagpole, where the Southern Cross flag hung limply, I found John Joe.

'John Joe!' I ran to him. 'Oh, please be alive!' I knelt and held him to me. I pulled him even closer when I saw a pair of military boots stop beside me.

'Dead!' I cried as convincingly as I could. I looked up and saw the uniformed trooper, his bayonet poised to finish off the badly wounded. Then I gasped, as I recognised the young trooper whose glances had once made me happy.

'Dead,' I said again.

It was at that moment that John Joe groaned and opened his eyes.

Epilogue

'What is your grandfather up to, Esty?' Mama sighed. 'I have to write out the lunch menu.'

'Patience, Mrs Maher,' said May, putting down her basket and spreading her skirt as she sat on the sofa. She brushed the velvet collar of her tight-fitting jacket and looked at me. 'What do you think of my town outfit, Esty?'

I smiled, and nodded my head. 'Very elegant, May, just like every other outfit in your wardrobe. I sometimes wonder where Adam manages to keep his clothes.'

'Oh, men don't need as many changes as we women do,' May laughed. 'Besides, it's important for the wife of a prominent businessman to have a well-dressed lady on his arm.'

'Well, your house is certainly big enough to accommodate several wardrobes,' Mama put in, as she stepped out on to the balcony.

It was quite true. *Baker and Son, Master Butchers* was a fine shop, over which were roomy living quarters divided between May and Adam, Rose and James. It had been completed in time for the wedding almost one year ago. What an exciting, glorious day that had been!

A true Irish wedding in the heart of Australia! Grandpa had offered to lead May to the altar to give her away, but May had politely refused.

'I've asked John Joe to do that, Mr Maher,' she said. 'He was like a brother to me when I was in service, and a brother is the person who gives you away when you don't have a father.'

Now, when I looked at May, I marvelled at the seamless way she'd moved into a way of life so remote from tending the Burgess ladies. What a way we've come, I thought.

At first we'd been disappointed by the small amount of gold we harvested from our shaft before giving up.

'The gold,' Grandpa had said apologetically, when he counted out the money he'd received from that last nugget, 'is not the fortune we'd hoped for. But it will give us a step up.'

His words proved to be true. Mama had become so immersed in her catering business that she'd rented premises for a restaurant in Ballarat. With business booming, she was soon able to buy the whole property – over which we had spacious living quarters built in the colonial style, and a garden where she grew her vegetables and herbs. We'd agonised over an appropriate name, but it was Mama herself who'd come up with *The Bridge End Restaurant*.

'It was our address on the goldfield, and it will be our address now,' she said. 'We've crossed many bridges to achieve what we have, so the name will serve to remind us what we went through to find this happiness.'

Some of those bridges would haunt our dreams for years to come, but we had learnt to adjust to change and push the bad past aside. John Joe had made a good profit investing his money in some scrubby, seemingly worthless land beyond Ballarat, and was turning it into a successful horse-breeding business.

'Can you believe it, Esty?' he said, as he proudly showed me his property. 'My land, my horses. Just think – if I'd stayed in Ireland, I'd probably be dead.'

I still shudder at the word 'dead'. It's not death itself that disturbs me – it's the memory of that moment, etched in my mind, when I nursed John Joe on that awful morning and cried out 'Dead!'

The young trooper and I had looked at one another as John Joe groaned, injured – but very much alive.

Giles, for that was his name, leaned closer to me. 'Drag him to the barricade,' he said. 'I'll help.'

Thus, between the two of us, we dragged John Joe to a cart which had been appropriated for the dead. Giles stayed with me until the cart was pulled clear of the stockade. I'd wanted to thank him, but he'd simply nodded and backed away.

John Joe, being the tough survivor he'd always been, recovered after a few weeks – with just enough scars to boast about to anyone who'd listen.

Grandpa, along with Adam and the other stockade protestors, was jailed for several weeks, but they were all eventually acquitted when the miners' grievances were acknowledged and the law was changed. It was hard to believe, looking around our beautiful home and watching Mama bustling about her restaurant with such pride, that we'd once been so close to failure.

'Peter Lalor is on his way here for his morning coffee,' Mama called out, as she glanced down the street. 'What a shame to see his empty sleeve,' she sighed.

'It could have been worse, Mama,' I said. 'He's lucky he survived.'

I gave an involuntary shiver at the memory. As Giles and I carried John Joe towards the dead wagon, I caught a glimpse of Peter Lalor being dragged away by some of our own people. They got him to the safety of a priest's house, where his badly injured arm had to be amputated.

'Goodness, Mrs Maher,' said May. 'Did we ever think we'd see the day when a representative of...' she broke off and turned to me. 'What is he representative of, again, Esty?'

'Of the Miners' Legislative Council,' I laughed.

'Yes, that,' said May. 'Did we ever think that someone so important would be a customer of the grandest restaurant in Ballarat – owned by one of us?'

'Which makes a change from being a wanted man with a sentence of death hanging over him,' said Mama, coming into the room again. 'What is Father at, keeping us waiting like this? I cannot think what he's up to. He spends all his spare time in that locked shed at the bottom of the garden and he won't let the rest of us look inside.'

'He's probably making stools for the children,'

I said. 'I've heard him say that there are more pupils turning up.'

By day, Grandpa was working at something that had always been dear to his heart – teaching. He'd built a wooden school at the edge of town and rounded up the youngsters running amok around Sovereign Hill to give them an education. At first, most of them had resisted, but he'd gradually coaxed them in with the stories he read from his books. They were now well into learning to read for themselves.

'Help me, Esty,' he'd said. 'Between us, we could tame these wild youngsters into outstanding citizens.'

'No thank you, Grandpa,' I replied. 'Apart from the fact that those urchins terrify me, I'm much happier taming words. Words do what you tell them.'

But Grandpa, with the help of Peter Lalor, succeeded in raising funds for his school, and also in employing the enthusiastic Mrs Atkins, whose husband, Pastor Atkins, had died of fever leaving her penniless.

Surprisingly, she agreed with Grandpa that religion would not be part of their teaching.

'These children come from many lands with different faiths, my dear,' he'd said. 'We must not impose our doctrines upon them.'

'Indeed,' Mrs Atkins replied. 'We shall civilise them first, Mr Maher. That is surely our first duty.'

'Good morning.' A gentle voice broke into my thoughts.

The three of us turned towards the door. 'Oh, Mrs Casey,' Mama said, and patted the sofa. 'Come and sit down.'

'I've made out the day's menu in my head,' she said. 'I just need you to write it down.'

Mrs Casey. I took a deep breath of satisfaction as I watched her and Mama working together. My world was now complete. Mama's letter to Mr Egan a year ago had brought the troubled reply that Mrs Casey was about to be replaced by a younger cook. Mama had kept this information to herself, but as soon as she could, she had put things right by sending money to arrange assisted passage to Australia for Mrs Casey.

None of us had known anything about this until Mama took me to meet the stage coach twelve months later. I thought she was expecting a parcel – we often got things for the restaurant delivered by the mail coach.

I was struck dumb when I saw the familiar, plump form of Mrs Casey descending from the coach. Even as she stood looking about with a dazed expression, I could not grasp the reality of her standing here in Ballarat.

'Mama. That can't be…'

Mama laughed, and gave me a gentle push in the direction of the descending passengers.

'Mrs Casey,' I shouted, as I threw myself at her and felt her familiar comforting arms envelop me, just as they had long ago in her kitchen. She put her two hands on my face and beamed at me.

'It's you!' I exclaimed. 'It's really you.'

'And look at you,' she said. 'All grown up and brown as a berry. Where's my little Esty?'

'I'm still me,' I laughed, holding on to her stout body in case she'd disappear. Arm in arm, we walked with Mama back to the restaurant, asking questions about the homeland that had become a distant memory, and listening to her marvelling at the shops and fine buildings of Ballarat. I remember being almost afraid to go to bed that night, in case I'd wake up to find it all a dream.

'What a kind thing to do, Mama,' I whispered, when all the fuss began to die down. 'I can't believe…'

'Kindness?' Mama said with mock surprise. 'Nothing to do with kindness, Esty. I've been listening so long to your praise of Mrs Casey's cooking, that I decided I must have her for my restaurant.'

'But you arranged this long before you started the restaurant,' I put in.

'Ah,' Mama replied, her eyes twinkling. 'You see? I was planning this business from our first miners' dinner. I knew I'd found my niche even then.'

And indeed she had. She bloomed as she tended her customers, stopping to chat at tables and making her diners feel special with the personal touch of the proprietress. *Milady*, Grandpa called her.

She pretended not to like that.

'Will His Lordship be coming for Sunday lunch as usual?' May asked, with a mischievous smile that brought me back to the present.

'He's not a lordship, May,' I retorted. 'He's just

a third son who was pushed into the army even though he didn't want to. He won't even inherit…'

'Oh, poppycock, Esty,' laughed May. 'His pa's a lord, and that's grand enough, isn't it? You'll be a lady…'

'Stop, May!' I said. 'I'm almost nineteen, I have a career and I have no intention being either married or a lady. And don't you say anything, Mama,' I went on when I heard her chuckling. 'And that goes for you too, Mrs Casey,' I added, when I saw her eyes crinkle with mischief. 'We're just good friends, Giles and I. We just happen to work together.'

Which was how things had turned out. Giles had been invalided out of the army, after an injured knee on that fateful dawn had left him with a limp. He said it was the best thing – after me – that ever happened to him, since he hated the army. So we worked together on *The Ballarat Times*, when Giles wasn't working on his book on the Eureka Revolt.

Mama, Mrs Casey and May exchanged glances and smiled. 'You can still be a journalist with *The Ballarat Times* and be a lady,' said Mama.

'Mama!'

But Mama reached out and took my hand. 'We're just teasing, Esty,' she said. 'I'm so proud of you, I really am, each time I pick up the newspaper and see your name. Your papa would be so proud.'

Yes, I knew that. Many times I thought I could feel his influence as I wrote my articles. Papa's calm, steady outlook had stayed with me throughout those years. But I found it more and more difficult to remember his face.

There was a polite knock, and the kitchen boy stuck his head around the door.

'Mr Maher says, will you ladies join him in the garden, Ma'am.'

We followed him down the stairs. Grandpa was waiting in the garden. I was surprised to see Giles with him – he wasn't due for another couple of hours. I blushed.

Grandpa offered his arm to Mama.

'If Milady will be so good as to accompany me,' he said, with exaggerated grandeur.

Giles walked beside me as our small procession made its way to the end of the garden.

'What *is* going on, Giles?' I asked. 'Do you know? Are you part of this?'

Giles smiled. 'Perhaps,' he replied, 'I don't have the same amount of skill as your grandpa. But,' he added enigmatically, 'I like to think I helped in a small way.'

Grandpa stopped at the door of the shed and turned towards the rest of us.

'Let me say, first of all,' he said, 'that Giles and John Joe – who'll be along shortly – supplied the wood.'

'You were right, Esty,' May giggled in my ear. 'It's a set of wooden stools.'

With a flamboyant sweep of his hand, Grandpa ushered us through. Our silent disbelief was broken after a few seconds by a cry from Mama.

'My sideboard!' she gasped.

And so it was. Made with wood from Australian

trees, and complete with carved flowers, twisty pillars and mirrored back, it was almost a replica of Mama's old sideboard.

I gazed at all of us reflected there in the mirror.

Suddenly I knew I'd found the magical, back-to-front place that I'd dreamed about all those years ago.

Historical note

The Great Irish Famine of 1845-51 was caused by the repeated failure of the potato crop, Ireland's staple food. It devastated the Irish population. One million people starved to death, while a further million emigrated to America and Australia. Many died of disease on the overcrowded 'coffin' ships.

The Whiteboys were a secret society of young men who, in their uniform of white shirts, rebelled against the landlords who were forcing the rural poor from their holdings by imposing exorbitant rents.

In the 1850s, the Colony of Victoria was under British rule. When gold was discovered in Ballarat, the Governor imposed on the diggers an exorbitant monthly tax – the equivalent of a month's earnings – which they had to pay whether they found gold or not. In 1854, the tax collection was increased to twice a week. This, along with the fact that the diggers had no vote and, therefore, no say in the running of the diggings, led to the Eureka Stockade uprising.

In October 1854, a young digger called James Scobie was murdered outside the Eureka Hotel by the owner, James Bentley. The case against Bentley was dismissed by the magistrate, who was a friend of his. This infuriated the diggers, 4,000 of whom gathered outside the hotel to protest. They burnt the hotel to the ground.

Peter Lalor was born in Ireland in 1827. He graduated as a civil engineer from Trinity College, Dublin. He arrived in Ballarat in 1854. When he witnessed the injustice and hardship imposed on the diggers, he tried to improve their lot by peaceful means. But when more aggressive restrictions were imposed on the diggers and their protests continued to be ignored, he became one of the leaders of the Eureka Stockade.

The Eureka Stockade was erected at the end of November 1854, as a defence against the troops who were massing to imprison those they regarded as troublemakers. On the night of Saturday 2nd December, most of the diggers, who were not expecting an attack on the Sabbath, had left to spend time with their families. About 100 men were left guarding the stockade. Between 2 and 3 a.m. the troops and police charged. Over thirty diggers were slain. Peter Lalor was shot in the arm, but was smuggled away to the home of a Catholic priest, where his injured arm was amputated. The battle highlighted the injustice suffered by the diggers and resulted in their grievances being heard and acted upon.

Henry Seekamp was born in England. He became Editor of *The Ballarat Times*. His sympathies were with the diggers and, through his newspaper, he strongly criticised the Government's unreasonable treatment of them. He also exposed police harassment and corruption. After the battle at the Eureka Stockade, he was arrested. His wife was quoted as saying, 'If Peter Lalor was the sword of the movement, my husband was the pen.'

MARY ARRIGAN studied at the National College
of Art and Design in Dublin, at University College,
Dublin and at Florence University. She taught art for
18 years before starting to write for children. She was
awarded the International Youth Library (Munich) White
Ravens title in 1997 and the 2000 Bisto Merit Award.
She has written several novels for children. Her previous
book for Frances Lincoln was *Mario's Angels*,
illustrated by Gillian McClure. Mary lives
in County Tipperary, Ireland.